Unfeminine. U
Deep down, that was how she'd always seen herself.

Guys often came on to her; she'd never doubted she was physically attractive. But she had this awkward…fault.

On the rare occasions she'd let a guy close, the instant he kissed her she started worrying about her performance. Was she kissing him back hard enough? Being sexy enough? Pleasing him? What if they bumped noses?

But something was going wrong with Gar. Seriously wrong.

His mouth touched hers, first lightly, then playfully, before settling in for a savoring slow kiss. It was as if he had nothing more important to do with his time than stand there and kiss her, maybe forever.

And Abby suddenly forgot to worry about bumping noses….

SUPER ROMANCE

THE STANFORD SISTERS: Three sisters discover once-in-a-lifetime love and strengthen the bonds of family!

THE STANFORD SISTERS

Dear Reader,

As the long summer stretches before us, July sizzles with an enticing Special Edition lineup!

We begin with this month's THAT SPECIAL WOMAN! title brought to you by the wonderful Jennifer Greene. She concludes her STANFORD SISTERS series with *The 200% Wife*—an engaging story about one woman's quest to be the very best at everything, most especially love.

If you delight in marriage-of-convenience stories that evolve into unexpected love, be sure to check out *Mail-Order Matty* by Emilie Richards, book one in our FROM BUD TO BLOSSOM theme series. Written by four popular authors, this brand-new series contains magical love stories that bring change to the characters' lives when they least expect it.

Pull out your handkerchiefs, because we have a three-hankie Special Edition novel that will touch you unlike any of the stories you've experienced before. *Nothing Short of a Miracle* by Patricia Thayer is a poignant story about a resilient woman, a devoted father and a cherished son who yearn for a miracle—and learn to trust in the wondrous power of love.

If absorbing amnesia stories are your forte, be sure to check out *Forgotten Fiancée* by Lucy Gordon. Or perhaps you can't pass up an engrossing family drama with a seductive twist. Then don't miss out on *The Ready-Made Family* by Laurie Paige. Finally, we wrap up a month of irresistible romance when one love-smitten heroine impulsively poses as her twin sister and marries the man of her dreams in *Substitute Bride* by Trisha Alexander.

An entire summer of romance is just beginning to unfold at Special Edition! I hope you enjoy each and every story to come!

Sincerely,

Tara Gavin,
Senior Editor

JENNIFER GREENE

THE 200% WIFE

Published by Silhouette Books
America's Publisher of Contemporary Romance

SILHOUETTE BOOKS

ISBN 0-373-24111-9

THE 200% WIFE

This edition published by arrangement with Harlequin Books S.A.

Printed in U.S.A.

Books by Jennifer Greene

Silhouette Special Edition

†The 200% Wife #1111

Silhouette Intimate Moments

Secrets #221
Devil's Night #305
Broken Blossom #345
Pink Topaz #418

Silhouette Books

Birds, Bees and Babies 1990
"Riley's Baby"
Santa's Little Helpers 1995
"Twelfth Night"

*Jock's Boys
†The Stanford Sisters

Silhouette Desire

Body and Soul #263
Foolish Pleasure #293
Madam's Room #326
Dear Reader #350
Minx #366
Lady Be Good #385
Love Potion #421
The Castle Keep #439
Lady of the Island #463
Night of the Hunter #481
Dancing in the Dark #498
Heat Wave #553
Slow Dance #600
Night Light #619
Falconer #671
Just Like Old Times #728
It Had To Be You #756
Quicksand #786
**Bewitched* #847
**Bothered* #855
**Bewildered* #861
A Groom for Red Riding Hood #893
Single Dad #931
Arizona Heat #966
†The Unwilling Bride #998
†Bachelor Mom #1046

JENNIFER GREENE

lives near Lake Michigan with her husband and two children. Before writing full-time, she worked as a teacher and a personnel manager. Michigan State University honored her as an "outstanding woman graduate" for her work with women on campus.

Ms. Greene has written more that forty category romances, for which she has won numerous awards, including two RITA Awards for Best Short Contemporary Book, and both a Best Series Author and a Lifetime Achievement Award from *Romantic Times.*

Dear Reader,

I was especially delighted to have Abby included in the That Special Woman! program. She is the third sister in my Stanford Sisters trilogy, and when I conceived these three stories, I was thinking especially of all the new and changing roles for women today. We all seem to be too busy. We all seem to be struggling to find a balance in our lives, between the wonderful traditional roles—like mom and homemaker—and yet also seeking fulfillment in different ways than our mothers and grandmothers had the freedom to try.

Abby is one of the "strugglers." She's tried hard to be a superwoman—to do everything 200%—and when she discovers she is overweighing the role of a career in her life, she's determined to turn herself into a cookie maker and a pro at homemaking and crafts. The hero figures out long before Abby that she's not only lovable but "a special woman"—even if she is dangerous near a cookie recipe.

But that isn't so easy for Abby to see...like so many of us, she's trying her best to "do it all." For all of you who've ever struggled to find that right balance in your lives, I wrote Abby for you...and I hope you enjoy the story!

Jennifer Greene

Chapter One

Abby Stanford heard the muffled pop. She just didn't know what the sound meant.

In her typical fashion, she was driving fast—even on unfamiliar, snowy, twisting mountain roads at midnight. Her satin-black Lexus was made to take curves, and Abby did most things in life at rocket speeds. That was about to change. As of tomorrow, she planned an entire reprogramming of her personality—she intended to take up a lolling, decadent, lazy life-style—but first, she had to get to Tahoe. Maybe the trip from Los Angeles to South Lake Tahoe took the average driver eight hours, but she fully expected to make it under seven.

She was within twenty minutes of her destination. Neither a killer headache, exhaustion nor a little snowstorm had slowed her up so far. Compared to those three obstacles, the strange little popping noise seemed totally inconsequential.

Then she heard a new sound. Sort of a distant *gablub, gablub.* The car suddenly didn't want to steer straight. And the fanny of her Lexus seemed to be sinking on the right side.

She'd never had a flat tire and sure as peanuts had no patience or time for one now, but the *pop*-and-*gaglub* sequence seemed to point inexorably to that particular diagnosis.

Hands clenched on the steering wheel, she quickly glanced in the rearview mirror. No one behind her, no one ahead of her. U.S. 50 coming into Tahoe was normally a well-traveled road, but not this late at night, and not in a snowstorm. She swerved to the shoulder, pushed on the four-way-flasher button and resolutely stepped out of the car.

The cold was a shock of a slap. Snow instantly pelted her face and stung her cheeks. Her spectator pumps immediately sank in several inches of soft white fluff. When she left Los Angeles, the trench coat, over a business suit, had been ample weather protection, and yes, of course she'd expected colder temperatures in Tahoe. She just hadn't anticipated needing to get out of her warm car, except to walk to the condo she'd rented.

A bitter wind intimately crawled up her stockinged legs, dipped into the vee of her coat. Earlier, she'd seen the silver comma of a moon, but clouds scuttled thick and heavy overhead now. Still, visibility was no real problem, because the snow was as hard-bright as diamonds. Arms hugged around her chest to keep warm, she tromped to the rear of the car and studied the back tire from one angle, then another.

Every angle looked the same. The tire had a lot in common with a beached whale. It wasn't just flat. It was totally-dead-flat.

She ran a hand through her hair and swallowed hard. Panicking was out of the question. She never panicked, and even if she was slightly tempted, falling apart would simply have to wait until she had time. Calling for help was not an option. For the past seven years, Abby had practically been connected at the hip to her cellular car phone, but the darn phone was just one more symbol of the overbusy life-style she wanted to put behind her. She'd gotten rid of it—a little too soon, she recognized with dark irony. More to the immediate point, no lights or buildings were in sight, and she hadn't seen another motorist in miles.

Every way she assessed the situation, she simply had to solve this one on her own, and that was that.

Sinking and slipping in the snow, she fumbled with the car keys and opened the trunk. Since she'd packed for a two-month stay in Tahoe, the trunk was predictably stuffed to the gills. She hurled one Bill Blass suitcase in the snow, then another, then a third. That cleared out the bulky debris. Somewhere in the rest of the mess, she knew, the trunk held a flashlight. A spare tire. And a jack.

All she needed to change a tire.

Assuming she knew how.

Abby swallowed again, but there seemed to be a lump in her throat the size of Utah. It didn't want to go down. Her pulse was rush-and-gushing adrenaline, her head throbbing from an exhaustion headache. The problem, she told herself firmly, wasn't being scared out of her mind. The problem was attitude.

It was January 1—her thirty-fourth birthday—and the whole world had crashed on her a week ago. She'd started this trip with the nasty little word *failure* bleating in her heart like a lost lamb. When a woman lost everything that mattered to her, she was entitled to be a bit touchy. She was even entitled to a mood rivaling a snarling pit bull's.

But a bad attitude wasn't getting the job done. Abby had always loved challenges, thrived on stress, expected competence from herself. The situation simply called for a self-administered kick in the rump. This was just a stupid flat tire, for Pete's sake.

Anyone could cope with a flat tire.

She clamped her jaw tight. And moved. The bottom of the trunk was tomb-dark, but she found the flashlight and flicked it on. There was no spare tire in sight, but the flashlight beam revealed a platelike thingamabob. Her fingers turned numb-cold as she battled with the plate thingie, and presto, just beneath it was the spare.

The spare looked significantly smaller than the real tire—which Abby assumed would make lifting it out easy. Unfortunately, her slight five-foot-four-inch frame was short on ballast, and her frozen feet, in heels, gave her no traction at all. Eventually she managed to heave the sucker into the snow next to her suitcases.

Out of breath, her headache screaming, she turned her attention to finding the jack. Everyone knew you had to have a jack to change a tire. She had no idea what to do with the jack, but one problem at a time.

Anxiety was licking its chops, starting to stalk her heartbeat. Moving, not thinking, was best. Her feet and hands were stinging-cold now, and the silence and isolation of the mountain road were increasingly difficult to ignore. The car heater could keep her warm for a while, but she was near the end of her destination, and naturally low on fuel. Counting on heat from the car was just no solution. Either she licked this tire thing, and soon, or she could be in real trouble.

Her two sisters would definitely be upset if she froze to death. Paige was a new mom, Gwen a new bride. It was a rotten time to give either of them a problem, so Abby decided she simply wouldn't. It only took a hellaciously long five minutes before she located what she thought was the jack. The tool was nice and small and shiny-new—but when she tried lifting it, the jack wouldn't budge. It seemed to be locked in some way. Wrenching and tugging got her nowhere.

She swallowed hard. Again.

Scowling and muttering, she stubbornly hiked up her skirt and climbed into the trunk, bent over in the cramped space and started pulling at the jack again. She strained her shoulder and arm muscles. She swore. She gasped and grunted in her best imitation of a draft horse. The result was zip, *nada,* zero. Somehow, the jack was locked in there tighter than a bank vault. It didn't move. Even an inch. Even a fraction of an inch.

The humor hit her suddenly. Her sisters claimed she'd been a high achiever in diapers. Ambition had always motivated her. She could make a financial statement sing. She could put a ten-million-dollar ad campaign together overnight. She'd climbed the corporate ladder, competing with the toughest guys in the business, outworking and outfinessing the boys in the office and the boardroom. She'd never failed to ace a test en route to her M.B.A., and until recently—a week ago, in fact—she'd claimed a salary to make any average Joe salivate.

But somehow she'd never gotten around to learning anything so basic or normal as how to change a tire.

Was that funny, or was that funny? Talk about taking a wrong life turn. She'd always been so sure where she was going, but an M.B.A. and a mountain of ambition weren't worth a pile of horsefeathers at the moment. Maybe they never had been, and she was slapstick-tired, goofy-tired. A raw, dark chuckle erupted from her throat. The chuckle turned into a ragged-edged laugh as she climbed back out of the trunk and sank down on one of the suitcases. She just needed a second to recover from all this humor.

Snow swirled in her eyes, sharp and biting and strangely salty. She certainly wasn't crying.

Abby Stanford never cried.

You could take that one to the bank—and earn interest.

Garson Cameron noticed the black Lexus parked up ahead on the other side of the road, but paid no attention. He saw the four-way flashers, but no sign of a body in the car, and a stalled vehicle in snow country was hardly news. He was beat, morose and restless, a mood undoubtedly brought on by the brunette he'd just left. Narda was bright, attractive, invariably fun...and the only reason he was driving home instead of snuggled up in her king-size bed at this precise moment was because he was an idiot.

Gar valued honesty to a fault, always had. He and Narda had been unfailingly frank with each other. The relationship was going no farther than friendship, but she'd have settled for a sexual-friends twist in that road. She was a damn beautiful woman. He was horny as hell. He was tired of waking up alone; celibacy was making him testy as a crab, and he was damned if he knew why he'd turned her down.

At thirty-six, he seemed to be turning into a hard-core fuddy-duddy. Maybe he didn't love her. Maybe he'd lost interest in sleeping with a woman when there was no risk or challenge of serious investment in the ante. But it was twenty-two degrees, it was snowing like the devil on a witchy-black, lonely night, and for damn sure principles weren't gonna keep him warm.

A man who took principles too far, Gar thought darkly, was stupid. By now, if he'd stayed, the two of them could be...

His Cherokee was just passing the black Lexus when he caught a sudden flash of color and movement. The vehicle had looked clearly abandoned from the front—but damned if there wasn't a woman behind the car. A blonde. Sitting on a stack of suitcases in the middle of the snow.

And as far as he could tell, boo-hooing her eyes out.

Hell. The sexual fantasy about Narda died a fast—and unwilling—death. He slowed down and shifted in his seat, an exasperated scowl directed at the rearview mirror. The hour was already barreling after midnight, the temperature was colder than a well digger's ankle, and the woman would probably be more scared than grateful if a strange man stopped to help. He'd be home in ten minutes, could call the police from there. There was no reason he had to play Good Samaritan.

But damn. It *did* look like she was crying.

A second later, the road curved, and she was out of sight. Possibly because it was his night to earn a Ph.D. in stupidity, Gar's foot tapped the brake.

Muttering a train of colorful insults—all self-directed, all deserved—he turned the Cherokee around and drove up behind her. Not too close. He wasn't necessarily committed to stopping, just to getting a better look. Before his headlight beams caught the back of her head, he lowered the lights, and then hit the window button.

The sound reached him first. He could hear her crying even over the sound of the car engine. She wasn't wasting any time with any sniffly little tears, but indulging in a serious, down-and-dirty crying fest with gusto. Not good news, but at least Gar had no reason to worry that she was physically hurt. It took energy, if not downright strength, to cry that loud.

"Miss? You need some help?"

Her head jerked up and around. Even with the midnight sky roiling with snow clouds, there was ample light to garner a basic look at her. She was young. Late twenties? Her hair was damp, shoulder-length, glinting like wet gold. There were too many shadows for him to tell if she was pretty, but it was easy enough to see that she lacked any sense or sanity.

Upscale trench coat. No hat. High heels, no boots. Wind chill hovering around zero, with four feet of snow piled on the banks, and she was dressed for a board meeting. Gar sighed—an exhausted sigh that any other man would have readily understood. In any other circumstance, he could have left her, gone home, called the cops or a tow truck or someone else to rescue her. But there was just no way even a conscienceless cad could desert a woman this dumb.

Leaving the heat and engine running, he opened the door and peeled out of the truck. Before his boots hit the ground, he was scanning the scene. "So what's the trouble? Engine die, or did you get stuck in the snow, or—?" Before he finished the questions, his gaze pounced on the flat tire—and the spare by her feet. Her car problem was obvious, but another glance at her established the only immediate priority. "You need to get warm and dry. Fast. Just quit crying, okay? Nothing to be scared about, everything's gonna be all right—"

"I'm *not* crying." She was on her feet in a shot. "I was just stopping to rest for a minute because I had such a terrible time getting the jack out and I—"

"Uh-huh." By his definition, she'd been wailing loud enough to start an avalanche, but Gar wasn't about to call her on the fib. Since she'd already incontestably established her lack of I.Q., he couldn't see wasting time arguing with her either. "Let's get you in my Cherokee. The heater's already on, and there are blankets in back, so we'll get you warm in no time—"

"I *have* to fix the tire."

"I'll fix the tire."

"I can *do* it. I just couldn't figure how to get the jack out—"

"Uh-huh." He didn't interrupt her again from rudeness, but from necessity. The faucet was pretty well shut off, except for some sniffly hiccups, but her teeth were chattering so hard she could hardly talk—which didn't, Gar noted, stop her from trying. In case she didn't notice which of them was six-foot-three and two hundred and twenty pounds, he used his clearest cut-to-the-chase tone. "This is what we're doing. You're getting in my Cherokee and you're getting warm—right now. If there's any slim, remote chance you've got a real coat or warm clothes in those suitcases, I'll bring 'em over and you can change in the truck—"

"Yes, of course, there's all kinds of clothes in my luggage, but—"

"I'll tell you what. You can argue with me after you get warm and dry, okay? All you want. And I realize you can't be in a hustle to get in a strange vehicle with a man you don't know from Godzilla, but you see the logo on the Cherokee's door? Cameron Crest Ski Lodge. That's me. Gar Cameron. I can show you a driver's license if you want, but honest to Pete, think about it—if I were any kind of self-respecting serial killer, I'd be home in bed with a book on a night like this. So just try and trust me, okay?"

He thought a little low-key patter might reassure her, but abruptly his voice trailed off. He was closer to her now. Close enough to feel a punch in his gut at the look of her. The phrase *drowned rat* came to mind. She was built delicate, no spare bulk anywhere. Her hair was slicked to her scalp, and except for burning-red cheeks, her skin was whiter than parchment. Still, those huge dark eyes were so riveting they damn near took his breath. She was so cold she was weaving on her feet, unsteady, tottering on those stupid high heels.

Discussion time was over. "I'm carrying you to the truck," he said gruffly.

"No, of course you aren't—I can walk."

He figured the chances of her making it to the Cherokee alone were five, six million to one. But he was wrong. Maybe it was that stubborn, contrary nature of hers giving her strength, but he flanked her slip-sliding path back to his Cherokee. She stumbled, but she made it. He opened the driver's door, gave her fanny a boost inside—nothing personal—and then shoved her over so that he had space to climb in and flick the heater switch to high. "You just stay up here in front. Get those damn wet shoes off—and the stockings, too."

He leaped out, hiked around to the back, and started pulling out lightweight silver survival blankets from his emergency kit. Carrying those and a brandy flask, he headed back for the driver's seat—keeping his eyes averted.

"Take anything wet off first. Then wrap up in the blankets. Then the brandy—but no more than a couple slugs. No matter how many times you've seen it on TV, liquor's a lousy idea for any kind of shock—but what you want is something with a sugar content, and that's the best I've got."

Without waiting for her to comment, he left again, stomping back in the snow for her luggage. No question she was pure female. All three of them were packed with rocks. He carted them over, this time using the side door. The back seat area at least had some space to maneuver around. "Okay, now just tell me which one has some warm clothes—Papa Bear, Mama Bear, or the baby carry-on?"

"The big one."

Naturally. Tough to do anything in the dark, tougher yet to juggle the brick-loaded monster sucker on top, then to get it open. Perfume wafted out. Feminine. Expensive. Spicy. The scent charged straight to his masculine hormones, a response he appreciated about as much as a dog bite. From a yapping terrier.

Even the dark shadows picked up the glow of satin lingerie. He didn't see any wool socks.

"You don't have to do that. I can..." she began.

Her voice was a husky alto—still raw and shaky with cold. He guessed she was pushing hard on any strength reserves she had left. "Look, I know this has to seem intrusive, but the faster we get you warm, the better. And all I'm doing is finding something warm and dry for you to put on."

The task was easier said than done. He didn't want to turn on the overhead light while she was stripping off clothes, but it was too dark to really see. Intimately dark. Particularly as his hand pawed through slippery silks and straps and a bunch of terrifyingly fragile lace. Dammit, he should have slept with Narda. He could have had sex—probably twice by now—and had nothing more troubling to deal with than regrets in the morning.

His fingers grappled with some wool fabric. Whatever the clothes item, it was the closest he'd found to practical. He hurled it over the front seat.

"Thanks."

Socks followed.

"Thanks again."

At the bottom—naturally, the pit bottom—were boots. Suede, sheepskin lining. The style might be hopelessly silly, but they actually looked warm. "No coat?" he asked.

"Oh. I forgot. I have a jacket and coat in the back seat of my car, hanging up—"

"No sweat." He zigged to her Lexus, zagged back to the Cherokee with a pastel down jacket in tow. "Okay. You starting to warm up now?"

"Yes. Thanks. I..." Finally, there was color in her voice again. A throaty, soft woman color. "I'm sorry, Mr. Cameron. I should have thanked you right away for stopping—"

"Make it Gar. And you were cold and wet and shook up. I understood."

"I am grateful. Seriously—thanks."

"Seriously—you're welcome." For a minute, Gar wasn't sure how much or how long she'd been suffering from exposure, or if it was all right to leave her. But she seemed okay now. More to the point, her scent, the silks, and knowing she was rustling around in the front seat, stripping down and changing clothes, meant it was definitely a good idea for him to get out of there. "Look, you just stay in here and keep warm," he ordered her abruptly. "I'm headed out to deal with the tire."

The blast of frigid air hit him like Rolaids relief. Damned if he could explain the drumroll of hormones beating in his blood. Yeah, celibacy had been chafing on his nerves, but Gar was a long way from a teenage boy who got turned on by thin air. He'd never even caught a real look at her face. This was a rescue mission, not a party. His awareness of her was embarrassingly inappropriate and—considering how many women Gar had been around in his thirty-six years—confounding.

Well, whatever. The cure for his brief problem with insanity was at hand. The physical exertion required to change a tire—and a few minutes away from *her*—were just what the doctor ordered.

He got the jack out and set up. But the Cherokee's door opened before he had the first lug bolt loosened.

So much for Rolaids relief. Not that Gar looked up. "You don't need to be out here and getting rechilled all over again. This is just going to take me a few minutes. Go back inside the truck."

"I was going to stay there," she immediately assured him. "But the thing is, I'd never have been in this trouble if I'd just known how to change a tire."

"Look, miss...ma'am...?" Gar heard himself verbally fumbling, suddenly aware that he had yet to catch her name. But when he straightened up and turned, he forgot the question.

Before this, she'd been either moving or crying or in the pitch-black Cherokee, and he really hadn't caught a good look at her. Whatever she wore for makeup was long gone, and her hair was still damp. But those riveting dark brown eyes would make any man pause. The sweep of high cheekbones were rouged from the wind. The classy little nose, the arched brows, a mouth softer than whipped cream, and those dangerous eyes...abruptly Gar felt virtuously justified in having felt that drumroll of hormones.

It didn't *matter* that she was striking as sin. It didn't change what was happening here—which was nothing more than him playing a fast white knight to her flat tire. But a guy would have to be in a coma not to notice.

She supplied her name. "Abby. Abby Stanford."

"Okay. Abby. Now don't take this wrong. I'm not coming from a sexist attitude, but it takes some size and strength to change a tire—and that's just as true for a man as a woman. Your best bet for road trouble is having a cellular phone in your car to call AAA or a garage."

"Well, that's not only good advice, but I've been kicking myself for just getting rid of a cellular phone. Believe me, I'll get another one. But in the meantime...could I just watch, so at least I'll know how it's done?"

There seemed no harm in agreeing to that, but her definition of "just watching" had a lot in common with her bold-faced lie about not crying. Faster than he could raise an eyebrow, she was snuggling her fanny between him and the wrench. She just wanted to "try it," so she'd know "how it was done."

When he started to pull off the tire, she hunkered down and pulled with him—grunting like a seasoned mechanic. When he reached down for the spare, she was right there, scrabbling in the snow, reaching for it with him. When he started tightening down the spare, her hair whispered in his face as she angled closer to see—and then to take over.

A job that should have taken five minutes lasted a freezing, wind-whipped fifteen. She had more questions than a pesky child, absorbed his answers like she expected to be tested later. It was just a tire. Minutes before, she'd been badly chilled; those killer eyes had bruise-shadows. She looked more fragile than a hot-house orchid, and she admitted having spent the past seven hours behind the wheel, driving from Los Angeles, so she had to be beyond exhausted. But the lady just wouldn't give up.

He wasn't sure if she tickled his sense of humor or exasperated him, but he'd positively never met anyone quite like her.

Finally, the tire job was done, the tools were put away, her luggage was stowed back in her car. "You don't want to drive too far on that spare. I don't know where you're headed—"

"Silver Valley Road—it's on one of the South Lake Tahoe keys? I rented a condo there—"

"Yeah, I know the road. You're only about fifteen minutes away." He considered. "Your spare looks good, that's a reasonably short drive, and I don't know where you'd find a garage that's any closer—much less that's open this late. But it wouldn't be that far out of my way to follow you home. I'll give you the name of a garage to contact tomorrow for a new tire."

"Thanks, I'd appreciate that, but honestly, you don't have to follow me—"

Yeah, he did. She was stubborn and striking and a damned interesting woman, but Gar still wasn't absolutely certain she had the I.Q. of a turnip. It had nothing to do with her personally. It had to do with him, needing to go home and get some serious sleep before a long workday tomorrow. And he wasn't going to sleep—not well—if he was worried about her.

So he trailed her. The place was typical of the rented condos on the Tahoe keys, pricey, two layers of stone and wood, lots of windows, a fancy door. An upscale hideaway paradise. Nothing wrong with it—the place was a little beauty—but the windows were like black mirrors, and the place was as dark and silent as a cave.

He left the Cherokee's engine running, and hustled out to help carry in her luggage. She predictably protested. "You've done so much already, and I can handle it—"

"Just want to be sure you get in safely. You've got a key? And you know if the heat or electricity's turned on? If you have a working phone?"

A sudden smile. The first he'd seen. Just a little one, but winsome with honest humor, and what that smile did to her face wasn't a fair thing to do to a tired, vulnerable man in the middle of the night.

"Good grief, I really gave you a first impression of being a cream puff, didn't I? And I admit I was a mess when you found me with that tire, but I swear I'm more related to a tough cookie than a cream puff—in fact, I've been criticized half my adult life for being *too* tough. I'm grateful you stopped to help, and I appreciate it, but honestly, you don't need to worry about me. Thanks again, okay?"

Her "okay" was clear permission for him to vamoose.

As Gar barreled out of her driveway and aimed for home—at vamoose speed—he erased the lady from his mind. He'd done his rescue thing. Earned his Galahad medal for the day. He needed to feel no further responsibility for her.

Still, that tough-cookie label played back in his head. The woman he'd seen bawling on the side of the road wasn't remotely related to tough...and that last smile of hers had been as breakable as china.

She'd been criticized for being *too* tough? Her? The shrimp with the haunted eyes?

The tough-cookie tag would be downright funny, if it wasn't...mystifying.

Good thing, Gar told himself, that neither Abby's mysteries nor anything about her life were any of his business. She was interesting. The whole encounter had been interesting. But he hadn't reached the great age of thirty-six without recognizing when a woman was potential trouble.

He doubted there was a chance in a thousand of his seeing her again.

Chapter Two

Abby peeked through the window as the Cherokee backed out of her drive and disappeared into the snowy night. Whew. She hadn't run across many white knights in the corporate world—zero, at last count—but Gar Cameron would have headed the list if she had one. Disheveled glossy black hair. Eyes bluer than sky. The height and build of a football tight end—and he'd had a memorable tight end to go with it. A deep, gentle voice made to soothe a woman, or stir her up—either option being damned pleasant to fantasize about.

Her racing heartbeat summed it up. He was a hunk. And an extremely successful hunk, which she could have guessed from the way he moved and behaved, even if she hadn't noticed the logo on his truck. Gar was on top of his world.

An outstanding reason to obliterate the man from her mind—particularly now.

Swiftly she locked the door, peeled off her jacket and started switching on lights. This place was going to be her home for the next two months. Any other time, she'd have gotten a tickle out of prowling and exploring. But that would have been before she was fired. Before the word "failure" had become a threatening, frightening, sneaky little dragon that attacked her every damn time she was alone.

Turning on lights helped. So did finding a cordless phone. Before even heeling off her boots, Abby dialed her youngest sister in Vermont. It was only five in the morning there—a disgraceful time to call anyone—but Paige was usually up really early with the baby. More to the point, Paige would have a stroke, if not a tantrum, if Abby didn't report in. Both sisters knew she'd made the long drive from Los Angeles to Tahoe alone. Being the oldest, Abby was traditionally the problem-fixer and advice-giver of the trio, but lately...well, nothing had been the same lately. And Paige, for sure, would worry if she didn't call.

The phone only rang twice—enough time for Abby to tuck the phone in her ear, start carrying luggage and put on her peppiest, most cheerful voice. "I'm here, I arrived safely, the black-and-white cameo you sent for my birthday is the most gorgeous thing I've ever seen— God, are you talented, sis. And if I woke you up calling this early, I'm gonna kick myself in the keester."

Paige's laughter bubbled out, familiar, warm. "Glad you like the cameo, and of course you didn't wake me up. Your new niece likes to party at the crack of dawn.

In fact, I'm nursing Laurel right now. So the long drive went okay?"

"No sweat. Just took me a little longer because I ran into a little bit of snow."

"What's the place like?"

"Well, I'm just walking through it now, but it's about what I expected. Think I told you, I rented it through a real estate agent. The owner's a pilot, rents the place out during the ski season..." Still juggling luggage and the phone, Abby peeked in doorways as she talked, delivering a running report to keep her sister entertained.

"The living room's turquoise and stone, beamed ceilings, a fireplace flanked by French doors leading onto a deck. I'm really gonna suffer—there's a high-tech boob tube, stereo equipment, every creature comfort known to man and then some. There's an office–dining room and a bath downstairs, then the kitchen... It's got a TV, too, gorgeous appliances, a freezer big enough to hold a cow or two, black glass table. I think my pilot landlord must be a pretty strong party boy, because he's got more wineglasses than dishes, but what the hey? I could get into some lolling, lazy decadence for a couple of months...."

"Big talk for a woman who gets giggly on a single glass of sherry," Paige said dryly.

"That sounds suspiciously like an insult."

"Of course it's an insult. I'm your sister. And don't get bogged down insulting me back—I want to hear more details. What's the rest of the place like? There's an upstairs?"

"Yup." By then, Abby had padded up the teal-carpeted stairs and dropped two pieces of luggage. As soon as she switched on lights, she started reporting again. "One holy-cow bathroom, a square lapis lazuli tub big enough for two, Jacuzzi, phone, music piped in... The next time I call you, trust me, it's gonna be from that bathroom. In fact, if I ever get in that tub, I may never leave, just have Chinese delivered right here—"

"Yeah, yeah, what else?"

"Two bedrooms. One's locked—that's where the pilot guy keeps his personal things when he rents the rest of the place out. But then... Sheesh."

"What? What!"

Abby had almost dropped the phone when she flipped on the light switch in the far room. "The master bedroom's a seducer's lair," she said wryly. "Platform bed, one mirrored wall, royal blue carpet, blue satin sheets, fake-fur spread. Eek. We're talking *sybaritic* in capital letters. Pretty hard to sleep in here and dream of Bambi. On the other hand, the mattress is hard, and it's got a fantastic walk-in closet..."

"Abby?"

"What?"

"You're laughing and talking like normal," Paige said gently. "How about if we skip the chitchat and cut to the chase. Are you all right?"

Abby chugged back downstairs and brought up the last suitcase. "Sure, I'm all right. I'm hunky-dory—"

"And cats fly. When are you really going to tell me what happened with the job and that promotion?"

Mentally Abby damned all sisters—and hers in particular. She considered herself a *good* liar. Skilled. Imaginative. Experienced. But fooling a sister was tougher than selling swampland in Montana—not that she was through trying. "I already told you what happened. I didn't get the promotion," she said lightly.

"Yeah. I know what you said. I also know how you were at Christmas, all excited and high as a kite about this big promotion coming up. You go home to L.A., and then suddenly you're taking off to live in Tahoe for two months. And you want me to believe that everything's fine?"

As fast as a machine gun, Abby started opening cases and efficiently pelting clothes away in closets and drawers. "Everything *is* fine. I just needed a break—"

"Uh-huh. You either fill in the blanks or I'm gonna sic Gwen on you."

The threat of both sisters on her back was enough to upgrade the quality—and speed—of her fibs. Her voice immediately turned cool, calm and soothing. "Honestly, it was nothing more than a disappointment. When the CEO retired, I had a shot at the job. Yeah, I thought I'd earned it. I'd outworked and out performed every guy in the office, brought in twenty million bucks in accounts last year. The only cards stacked against me were that I was young and female. Age didn't seem that important. In the advertising business, everyone's young, because it's such a high-burnout field—"

"But they gave the job to a man?" Paige asked.

"Yes. An outsider. Fresh blood. That's just the way it's done sometimes. And you're not in business, but it's pretty standard procedure for a new broom to sweep out the old chaff—particularly if the old chaff was direct competition for his job. It wasn't personal. It's just business. And it's not like I'll have any problem getting another job. I've got unbeatable references, had four offers almost before I cleared out my desk—"

"I don't doubt that, sis."

"I just thought some time off would be a good idea. I haven't taken a real vacation in years. I didn't know this plum of a place would be available when I called the real estate agent, but it was. And Tahoe's gorgeous. And I've got a ton of money saved. So there was just no reason not to take a little break."

"You're telling me that's all she wrote," Paige murmured.

"Yeah. Everything's Georgy peachy. Honest."

Paige said patiently, "You're full of horse patooties, sis. But I'll let you be for now. You have to be exhausted after that long drive, so catch some sleep, and I'll call you in a couple of days."

When the phone connection was severed, the unfamiliar condo echoed with a sudden lonely silence.

Fired. Failure. The words whispered in her mind, like a shadow waiting to catch up with her, or like an alligator under the bed that only showed up when she turned off the lights and was alone.

Quicker than a mail clerk, she filed the last of her clothes in drawers and cupboards, thinking that at two in the morning—after a monstrously awful day—she should be more than ready to crash. But then she came across the last item packed in her suitcase. The boxed present Paige had sent for her birthday.

She sank on the bedspread and opened the box. Her sister was a gifted cameo maker, and the present was a sculpture, oval-shaped, an onyx-and-pearl cameo. The pearl-white profile of a woman was uniquely striking against the black onyx background. Abby set it on the teak bedside table, studying it with a fierce, painful lump in her throat.

Her youngest sister knew her so well. Maybe like only a sister can know another sister. Her whole life, Abby knew she'd tended to see things in black and white. Because she'd always been driven by ambition, she'd applied 200% of herself in that direction. She was a perfectionist and an achiever and a competent woman.

Failure had never been built into the picture. It couldn't happen. She'd never failed at anything.

But she'd failed now. And the whole rug of her life felt swept out from beneath her. The scary thought kept sneaking into her heart that she'd sold herself a line, that her whole life had somehow, innocently, mistakenly, become a lie.

She'd lost a job, and she'd told herself a dozen times that it was *just* a job. But her whole life had been defined by her career. She had the "right" apartment with a closetful of the "right clothes," and a living room decorated with the "right" colors and styles suited to an upwardly mobile executive. None of that had ever been fake. It was just that everything she made herself into had had the goal of success in her career, and now that she'd failed at that...none of it had any meaning.

And neither did she. The paralyzing thought kept flashing through her mind that she'd sold herself a lie. Success had mattered to her so much that she sacrificed her entire personal life to that goal. She couldn't shake the feelings of failure—as a person, and especially as a woman.

Abruptly she sighed—loudly—vaulted off the bed and started peeling off her clothes. God knew, it was tempting to beat herself up some more, but it really was late. As much fun as this self-beating-up routine was, it would wait until she'd caught some sleep.

She dug out a nightgown, switched off the lights and then dived for the depths of the giant platform bed. Unfortunately, the silly satin sheets were not only slippery but colder than ice. Her eyes popped right back open, and instantly she was wide awake again... and as sneaky as bad news, Gar Cameron's face scooched back into her mind.

Now *there* was a man to warm up a girl's sheets, an enticing fantasy to fall asleep on. Except that the memory clinging in her mind was of her making a fool out of herself, crying in front of a stranger...and her failure to cope with something so basic as a flat tire seemed a painful example of everything that was wrong with her life.

Well, that was precisely why she was holing up in Tahoe. To give herself time to change.

Resolve and determination had always been her strong points. Come daylight, she was going to start the process of turning her life around. She was going to change herself. Totally. Completely. 200%.

So long, Ms. Abby Workaholic Stanford. Whoever that woman was, she was about to be obliterated from the map. Abby had always faced her mistakes, chin up. If she could learn to run an ad agency single-handed, she could sure as hell learn to relax. As of the next morning, she intended to become a devil-may-care, disgracefully lazy sloth.

Or die trying.

* * *

Gar climbed out of the Cherokee with a scowl. It was a white-satin afternoon. The blazing sun had frosted a glaze on the fresh snowfall, and skiers at the lodge were crowding the slopes in a frenzy to enjoy it. He'd be enjoying it, too—if he could have gotten his mind off that damn blonde.

His eyes narrowed on her Lexus—she clearly hadn't moved it since last night, because the car had a whipped-cream coating from last night's snowfall. As he hiked toward her door, he considered that he had a perfectly reasonable excuse for stopping by. He knew her address, but not her phone number, and he'd neglected to give her the name of a garage where she could get a good new-tire deal.

The excuse was as lame as a politician's promise, and Gar wasn't particularly fond of making a fool of himself—but it was her own damn fault he was here. It had nothing to do with her gorgeous eyes or his frustrated hormones. At three in the morning, he'd been pacing around, remembering how hard she'd been crying on the side of the road. How vulnerable she'd been. How fragile and breakable she'd looked. How mule-headed-stubborn she'd been tackling the damn tire, beyond all reason or sense. And he'd just felt wrong about dropping her off at the dark, cold condo without knowing if the place was remotely livable or if she was all right.

He reached the carved oak door and rapped hard with his knuckles. That was all he wanted to know—if she was okay. A look at her would do it. Then he'd split. If his excuse of giving her the name of a garage place sounded hokey, what difference did it make? He'd be gone in two seconds....

At least that was the plan.

But the door was suddenly hurled open and she was there, barefoot, in jeans, wearing a cherry-red sweatshirt so oversize that two of her could have fit inside. A fine white dust coated the shirt, her cheek, her nose. Flour, he guessed, since she had a wooden spoon on one hand and a hot pad in the other. Her hair, such a glinting damp gold in the dark, was more taffy in daylight, as fine as silk, curling around her throat in a disheveled pageboy.

"Mr. Cameron—" Her voice was breathless—she'd clearly run to answer the door—and those sexy dark eyes shot wide with surprise when she recognized him.

"Gar," he corrected her, and swiftly hustled into his pitch. "I don't want to bother you. But I didn't know your phone number, and I promised you last night I'd give you the name of a reliable place where you could get that tire taken care of—"

"Well, heavens, that was nice of you to stop. You didn't have to go to all that trouble— Oh, cripes!" A buzzer caterwauled from another room. She lifted a hand in an exasperated gesture, but she seemed to have forgotten the hand was gloved in a thick hot pad. She barely missed smacking herself in the eye. A nervous laugh seemed to bubble out of her. "I'm afraid I'm in a bit of a mess, making some cookies. You, um, have a fondness for chocolate chip?"

Were rivers wet? Did a man like sex? Did she expect a serious answer to a question like that? "If you're offering, I wouldn't turn one down."

"Well...come in."

He wasn't sure if he was being let in only because she was frantic to get to that buzzer before her cookies burned. He wasn't exactly sure why he came in, for that matter. In a blink, he could see she was all right. Not only did she look rested, she appeared to have more energy than a moving tornado. She looked about ten in those skinny jeans and bare feet, but his male antenna immediately recognized that there was no bra under that voluminous sweatshirt, and he caught a distinctive whiff of that full-of-hell perfume.

She was definitely a full-grown woman.

He tromped in as far as the kitchen doorway, thinking he'd just scratch down the mechanic's name and exit before he could catch the flu—or anything equally dangerous. But the condition of her kitchen totally distracted him. She flashed him a smile.

"I don't do this too often," she admitted.

"No kidding?" At some point, the kitchen had conceivably been pristine—oak cupboards with leaded glass, stove and two-door freezer, teal Formica counters that wrapped the room in a serviceable U, a pricey little chandelier centered over a black glass table. The chandelier still looked virgin-pure, but nothing else had escaped the shambles.

At least five bowls of varying sizes were filled with cookie batter. A few dozen were cooling on the counters on cookie sheets. Cupboards and drawers hung open. Drips and spatters of flour and batter had enthusiastically landed everywhere. Making cookies for her seemed to be a whole-body experience, and it appeared she wasn't even close to halfway through the project. "Are you baking for an army?" he asked dryly.

Another flash of a cheeky, mischievous grin. "Not an army, no. To be honest, I seem to be making a few more than I originally anticipated. It's all my sister's fault."

"Your sister," Gar echoed.

"Yeah. I have two. This recipe was my sister Gwen's, and I should have guessed that anything from her would have quantities to feed an entire neighborhood. She lives in St. Augustine...."

She was chasing around faster than a magpie, switching off the buzzer, removing another sheet of cookies, reaching into a bowl to mix another batch at the same time. And blithely spattering more batter and flour dust with every move she made.

"And then I have another sister, Paige, the youngest in the clan. She lives in Vermont, which is where the whole family started out. I've been living in L.A. for more than seven years now, though, so I haven't been around snow like this in a long time. I went out this morning, just for fresh air, found a little grocer at the corner, didn't even have to drive to get all the stuff I needed for the cookie recipe..."

"Uh-huh. You like to bake, do you?"

"Oh, yes." Her eyes shifted away from his faster than a card shark's at a poker table. "I find it's just the thing when I want to relax."

"Relax," he echoed.

"Yup. I used to be one of those hard-core workaholic types. Not anymore. These days I'm so relaxed and laid back that..."

Gar was fascinated, wondering where she was aiming with that whopper of a lie, but her voice trailed off in midthought. No surprise. She was charging around faster than a high-strung racehorse. Another tray of cookies went in. The spatula whirled like a pinwheel as she sliced cooling cookies off another tray. Then she was mixing again. "Good grief, I didn't mean to talk your ear off. There's coffee over there in the corner. Raspberry almond. And for heaven's sake, take a cookie."

He took three. She wasn't going to miss them. And then he peeled off his jacket and started rolling up his sleeves. "It looks like you could use some help here," he said tactfully.

"You like making cookies?"

Not like she did. But at the lustfully enthusiastic rate she was going, the kitchen might not be recoverable in her lifetime. "Lonigran's is on Pine Street. Best deal on tires, he won't cheat you, and it's just two turns from here, about a ten-minute drive."

"Oh, thanks a lot."

"I'll jot down the address on the back of a business card." His teeth crunched into a cookie. The chocolate was still warm. Almost as liquid and warm as her dark chocolate eyes. *Go home,* warned every well-honed masculine instinct in his adrenal system. The woman had a batty streak. Something about those eyes was suspiciously, worrisomely haunting. And she watched him chomp down on that cookie with one of those all-knowing, wicked female grins.

"So," she murmured, "chocolate's your downfall, is it?"

"I just haven't had a homemade cookie in a long time," he said defensively.

"Uh-huh." That grin was getting broader.

"I don't smoke. Rarely drink. Work hard, wash behind my ears, rescue stray dogs. Hell, I was such a model citizen I was boring myself to death.... You believe me, don't you?"

"Uh-huh."

"I had to find a vice. Who wants to be around a saint?"

"Uh-huh." She watched him engulf a third one. "How long have you been a hard-core chocoholic?" she asked genially.

"Damn it. My whole life. I can't shake it for love or money. I'm just crazy about the stuff."

Laughter pealed out of her. Not laughter at him, but with him. Gar told himself he didn't know her well enough to laugh, really laugh, with her. And Abby couldn't conceivably know him well enough to tease him.

But feeling natural with her didn't seem to take any effort. God knew what she planned to do with all the cookies, but they flipped and mixed and spooned side by side, bumping hips, bumping glances. There was a certain wariness in her eyes. Wariness, but awareness, too. The oven temperature wasn't the only cause for the heat charging around the kitchen.

He had to move faster than a comet to keep up with her. If time would have obliged him and just stood still for a couple of seconds, Gar figured, he'd have caught his breath, realized it was nuts to be making cookies with a stranger of a woman in the middle of a work day. Actually, he did realize it was nuts. He just didn't want to leave.

She chattered as fast as she moved, nothing personal

or prying, just a steady stream of life stuff. "You said you had a ski lodge?"

"Yup. On the Nevada side of Tahoe."

"I take it you love skiing? Been doing it long?"

"Had the business about five years, didn't know a ski pole from a stick when I started. The place more or less fell in my lap originally, as part of a business deal, a company in debt—the lodge was part of the debt owed. So I was stuck with it, but never really spent any time here until a couple years ago."

"Something made you change your mind?"

"Yeah. A divorce. And a major need to change the life road I was headed down."

"I can relate to that. Not the divorce—I've never been married. But the need to stop and take another look at the atlas, so to speak. I was positive what I wanted to do in my twenties. And I did it. But I was speeding down that road so fast that I was missing the scenery, making wrong turns, didn't realize I was aiming for a place I didn't want to be."

"Yeah, exactly." He didn't expect her to understand. In fact, she couldn't. Neither of them had really spilled anything threateningly close to personal—it wasn't that kind of conversation. But there was a flash of that troubled, haunted look in her eyes, a moment when she just looked at him, and then suddenly she doubled her frenetic pace, charging around the kitchen.

When the oven buzzer droned—for the millionth time—she scrambled to take out the cookie sheet. And he noticed the time. "It *can't* be four o'clock. I can't believe I've been here all afternoon—or that you didn't kick me out long before this."

"Oh, no. You're not getting out of here *that* easily, Gar Cameron."

"I beg your pardon?"

"You just wait a second before pulling on that jacket. You try and leave without taking a full plate of cookies and I'll strangle you with my bare hands. Cripes. There has to be something I can wrap them in, somewhere in this kitchen. Don't you move. You hear me?"

A finger was waggled under his nose. A slim, pampered white finger that was exuberantly caked with cookie dough. "Believe me, you've got me too scared to move," he assured her.

"Good. Power. Threats. I swear it's the only way to make a man behave. Now..." She hunched down, and eventually emerged with some plastic wrap from a bottom cupboard. Then she bounced to her feet and started foraging in one of the top cupboards. She started pouring a heap of cookies onto a turkey-size platter. The heap turned into a generous mountain.

"You could save a few for yourself," he said dryly.

"Well, I owe you more than cookies for helping me out last night. And besides that, you're the one with the addiction. I can't stand chocolate chip cookies."

He'd just yanked on his alpaca-and-leather jacket when he stopped. "You don't like chocolate chip? You made all these cookies and you don't even—"

"I know, I know. It's insane. But it's something I was determined to take up. Insanity. Silliness. Whiling away an entire afternoon doing something aimless and foolish for the sheer pleasure of doing something for no purpose other than fun." She sighed. "Trust me, I don't expect you to understand. I just wanted to do something...relaxing."

He hadn't seen her relax for two seconds in the past several hours. It was utterly mystifying that she thought she was. But whatever he understood or didn't—whatever this whole crazy afternoon had meant—she was standing next to him at that second. Still. Actually standing still.

He never *planned* to kiss her. But God knew, catching her when she was standing still for a moment was a rare thing that might never happen again.

He'd had fun. For a few hours, he'd forgotten his life, his work, every problem that had ever been on his table. He didn't know how she'd worked that kind of magic, but at thirty-six, he didn't find magic too often, anywhere in life. Her face was tilted up to his. Watery sunlight had trapped copper and gold on one side of her hair, sunlight that touched her small blade of a nose, the delicate line of her cheek. The small mouth, red as cherries, curved in the same delectable feminine smile that had been teasing his hormones all afternoon.

And he pounced.

Chapter Three

Abby saw his hand reach out. Warning bells pealed in her mind. She instantly sensed that Gar intended a pass—she could hardly have reached the vast age of thirty-four, much less thrived in the cutthroat business world, without perfecting a honed survival instinct about men. She wasn't the fumbling, bumbling type. She never had a problem handling herself, and averting trouble was always a better strategy than trying to wade out of mucky quicksand later.

Seconds before, Gar had pulled on his jacket, a clear sign that he'd meant to leave—wanted to leave—and that he'd only been distracted by a momentary impulse. Swaying him from that momentary impulse should have been easy. She had ample time to sensibly duck and run. Whole long seconds. And she meant to.

But he was so close that she suddenly felt crowded,

cornered by the scents of leather and alpaca wool and warm, virile male. She felt his big hand cup her neck, tilting her face to his. She saw those gray-blue eyes, his sudden intense frown—there was more potential trouble in those eyes than she'd seen in a month of Sundays, and that frown was just as worrisome. She saw that smooth, narrow mouth dipping down, aiming for her, the window light catching the sharply cut lines of his cheek and jaw and the shine of his unruly dark hair.

She had her lips already parted to smile, to make a joke, to divert this nonsense before it ever happened.

But then his lips touched down. Gentler than a spring wind. Tasting of chocolate chips, for sure, but also something deeper, darker, luringly sweeter. And her heart was suddenly fluttering like shaky butterfly wings.

Unfeminine. Unsexy. Undesirable. Deep down, that was always how she'd seen herself. Guys often came on to her; she'd never doubted she was reasonably physically attractive. But she had this awkward...fault. No laws or women's lib movement had ever changed how people really felt. Men were respected for having drive and determination. Not women. Ambition was valued in a guy, but there was something suspect and unwomanly when it showed up in a woman.

Men weren't the only ones carrying that prejudice around. Women did, too. Like her. And like a third-party voyeur, that flaw had always sneaked to the surface on the rare occasions she let a guy close. Even if the man was a darling, the instant he kissed her, she instinctively started worrying about performance. Was her breath clean? Was she kissing him back hard enough, being sexy enough? Pleasing him? What if they bumped noses?

But something was going wrong with Gar. Seriously wrong. Disastrously wrong.

His mouth first skimmed over hers, lightly, playfully, then settled in for a savoring slow taste. Very slow. His lips shaped to fit hers like the seam of a licked stamp. Concentrating, as if he had nothing more important to do with his time than stand there and kiss her, maybe forever, as if a blizzard-driven avalanche could threaten any second and he wouldn't give a particular damn.

She couldn't seem to remember that worry about bumping noses. She couldn't seem to even remember the test. The oak-and-teal kitchen, the zillions of cookies, the disastrous mess...it was all still there. There was no spring meadow, no sultry winds; she was no young, untried girl experiencing the wonder of kissing her best guy for the first time. This wasn't...simple. Kisses were never simple between grown-ups.

Yet it seemed simple. Easy. To just thread her arms around his neck and hold on. To inhale that magnetic virile power of his and just enjoy.

She hadn't felt young in forever. She hadn't felt free...maybe ever. His mouth lifted, but only the distance of a whisper. His eyes searched hers. A thumb traced the line of her jaw, her cheek, and then he ducked down for another sample of madness. A river of honey couldn't move this slow, and his mouth was softer than moonlight, and heady, like the thrumming beat in a wild, lonely love song.

She didn't know him, and she'd never once been suckered into buying swampland in Montana, but damn. Blood was sluicing through her veins in an exuberant, electric rush. He was making her feel high, giddy-silly high, barefoot-kite-flying high, and that was ridiculous. It was impossible. She *had* to kiss him back until she understood where this magic and madness were coming from. She'd never backed down from a problem yet—and she positively never backed down when she was afraid.

So she kissed him back. Only the magic and madness became even worse, much worse. He washed her tongue with his, took her mouth with greedy possession, swept his hands down her shoulders, her spine, in a roaming caress. His jacket crunched between them. Her feet ached from being up on tiptoe. Her mouth felt hot and wet and like it wasn't hers anymore, but had somehow been changed forever by those dark, soft, dangerous kisses of his.

When he lifted his head, damned if she knew why. She felt oddly dizzy and disoriented, as if she'd guzzled several glasses of champagne, when she rarely drank champagne and she never guzzled...anything.

"Abby?" he murmured.

Damn the man. There was a smile in his eyes. A wicked, down-and-dirty, I'm-having-a-great-time smile. And the only intoxicating substance anywhere in sight was him. "What?"

"The oven buzzer's been screaming for the last minute or two," he mentioned. One of his fingers was threading through a strand of her hair, as if that screaming oven buzzer were of no interest.

Saving the last batch of cookies was a handy excuse to whip out of his arms and jog over to the stove. The cookies emerged both looking and smelling on the scorched side. Not significantly different from how he'd made her feel.

"Abby, I really do have to go. Though God knows, my mind isn't on work. I'm real tempted to just go out and lay in the snow for a couple of hours," Gar murmured dryly.

Her eyes shot to his.

"Are we, um, still speaking?" he asked.

"No."

Her blunt, glowering "No" only seemed to put a new, fresh sparkle in his eyes. "Well, hell. I'd apologize if I was sorry. But I had a blast making all these damn-fool cookies with you—and that was the best kiss I've had in a decade." He scratched his chin. "Maybe longer. In fact, I'm still suffering from the effects. Maybe if we tried another—"

His gentle teasing was clearly an effort to make her feel comfortable, and drat the man, it was working. Abby couldn't remember the last time she'd been charmed by a man—and she didn't want to be now. She sighed, loudly. And shoved the plate of cookies into his hands. "Go away, Gar Cameron. Do me a huge favor and forget you ever met me, okay?"

"Speaking conservatively, I'm 500% sure that isn't going to happen," he said mildly.

"Well, that's the way it has to be. I haven't a clue how to recoup from anything that went this totally wrong so fast. I *had* to give you a first impression of being a dumb, ditzy blonde when you found me stranded on the road…then I get a second chance to redeem myself, and undoubtedly gave you the idea that I throw myself at men I barely know. This isn't going anywhere. It's hopeless. Just go home, would you? I know you have no reason to believe me, but I swear I'm not normally this goofy—"

"You're not goofy."

"I sure as hell have been. With you." She steered him firmly toward the door. "Goodbye, good luck, thanks for all your help, and if the Fates would just be kind, we'll never have to run into each other again."

"Abby." He accepted her herding him rapidly out the door. But something flared in his eyes. Banked, dark, quiet fires. He was more than willing to leave, quickly. He was more than willing to charm and tease But his gaze locked on her eyes for one last brief second. "We're going to run into each other again," he said. His voice was low, soft. And dead sure.

So dead sure that Abby impulsively, instinctively locked the door after him. Then leaned against it with an exasperated shake of her head. Her whole body felt flushed, her pulse was racing like a manic engine, her nerves were as rattled as if she'd tangled with a tiger.

There was, of course, a reasonable explanation why Gar provoked such befuddling behavior from her. She tangled with men all the time. But not intimately. She'd become a pro at avoiding intimacy, but that didn't mean she hadn't been chased—regularly and exhaustingly. The chasers predictably fell into categories: The guys who assumed her skill in business meant she was a tough broad. The guys who hoped they could climb to a promotion through her bedsheets. Or the guys living in the fast lane, who considered a speedy romp in the sack a stress release on a par with Valium.

There'd never been a man who came on to her just

from...play. Where there was no side agenda. Where there was absolutely nothing motivating a kiss—or a connection—but the sheer wicked wonder of chemistry.

And damnation, that man *was* a wonder of testosterone.

Impatiently Abby pushed away from the door and aimed for the kitchen, thinking, *Anyone but him.* Fun was okay. If she found a man she wanted to spend time with, that was more than okay. But not *Gar*—not a man who was obviously in business, and just as painfully obviously a success at it.

She had to get away from the business world completely, and coming across a maestro achiever was salt in her open wounds. Around Gar, or anyone like him, her recent personal failures seemed even more shaming.

But as she reached the kitchen, her spirits lifted. Her gaze pounced from the tipped bowls to the crusted cookie sheets to the blotches of coagulating cookie dough. Okay, so it was a Kodak-moment mess—but tarnation, she'd done it. Survived an entire afternoon of playing. True, she had no home for some fifty million cookies, but that was a minor detail. What mattered was that a leopard *could* change her spots. A workaholic *could* master the fine art of relaxing. The disaster was living proof.

She found a radio station playing rock and roll, turned the volume on high, filled the sink with sudsy water and boogie-woogied through the entire cleanup job. She tuned her mind off Gar. Or tried to.

When the kitchen was finally done, she switched off the light and decided to head for the Jacuzzi with a glass of wine and a book. Maybe a long, decadent, lazy soak would get her mind off that embrace. Off him. Off those huge, wild, strangely-wonderful emotions he'd provoked with that damn kiss.

She kicked off her shoes, thinking that he'd simply startled her. That was all. It wasn't that hard to write off her response to him as a fluke, something she could ignore and forget.

Only it bit. That he'd shaken her. That she'd lost herself for those few minutes in his arms, when that simply couldn't have happened. And Abby just never believed in turning her back on a tiger. Running away always turned a tiger into a threat. A problem that a woman didn't face, test and conquer was a problem begging to come back and haunt her.

There was no reason she had to see Gar again. But she had a bad feeling it was going to nag at her conscience...until she did.

So far it'd been a good day, but incessantly busy. Around four o'clock, Gar hiked to his office to steal a fast five minutes of peace. He'd just poured a mug of coffee when he glanced out the window...and abruptly put the mug down.

His office was located on the third floor, west corner, where windows gave him a prime view of the ski slopes and the lodge grounds.

Cameron Crest Ski Lodge was no competition for Squaw Valley or Heavenly. Heavenly, for example, had twenty-three lifts, three high-speed quads, seventy-nine trails, ranging from beginners to advanced. Gar knew all his competitors' statistics. There had been a time when he'd have given the big boys a run for their money, for the sheer fun and risk and challenge of taking them on. But he'd brought this place back from ashes—maybe because his life had been ashes when he took it over—and nothing had ever given him more satisfaction than his little stretch of mountain.

His stretch of mountain was crowded with bodies today. Temporarily, though, it was only one body on the slopes that kidnapped his attention. He could only see the woman's back, but certain things about her were familiar—the pale blue down jacket, the slight frame, the shoulder-length hair glinting like toasted gold in the sunlight. Lots of blond females out there, all of them trussed up in pricey ski jackets, but this particular woman had her hands on her hips as she studied the setup on the beginner's run. It was that hands-on-hips I'm-looking-for-trouble posture that made him think of Abby.

Three days had passed since he'd seen her, and still, he remembered the trouble she'd given him. They were both too old to start something unless they mutually agreed ahead of time about the finish line. Maybe he'd kissed her on an impulse, but he'd never meant more than a casual kiss. At his age, he damn well knew the difference. He'd never expected to laugh, so easily and naturally, with a woman he barely knew...and he sure as hell had never anticipated an embrace to heat up, reeling out of his control almost before he knew what hit him.

He forced his gaze away from the blonde, and scanned the rest of the view with shrewd business eyes. There were skiers everywhere, which was as it should be. Vibrant jacket colors flashed against the white-white ground, cheeks burned claret-red, skis hissed on the slopes with a spray of white powder behind them... The gondola was running smoothly, thank God, a range of all ages were clustered around the instructor on the novice hill, someone was taking a tumble on the intermediate slopes. Nothing unusual for a busy Friday afternoon.

When his eyes—accidentally—bounced back to the beginner's run, the powder-blue jacket had disappeared. He shook his head at his own idiocy. The chances of Abby showing up at his particular ski lodge had to be a zillion to one. And she'd been on his mind, obviously way, way too much, if he'd started imagining her.

"Gar?" Robb's bearded face showed up at the door. "Your ex is on line one. You want me to put her off?"

Robb was twenty-eight, had a build like a bear and a bushy black beard, and in a place where no one dressed more formally than in a ski sweater and Dockers, he was addicted to starched oxford shirts. Gar wouldn't have cared if he showed up in sweats. Robb was the best secretary he'd ever had, here, in Houston or anywhere else. "Thanks for the offer. I may need Scotch later, but I'll take the call," Gar said dryly.

No matter how much he trusted Robb, it went against the grain to pawn off a personal problem on an employee. In the past few weeks, there'd been a sudden burst of calls from his ex-wife. Gar gulped a sip of coffee, mentally braced, and then impatiently snagged the phone.

Janet's voice was as sweet and soft as a promise. "I'd like to see you, Gar."

He'd already heard this tune, and would rather go

through an IRS audit than play it again. "I don't think so."

"I've been clean for six months now—"

"That couldn't be better news. I'm glad for you, seriously. But we already talked about this. I'm not trying to be mean, but I just see no purpose in any kind of meeting."

"I'd like to think we could be friends. There was a time we were more then friends, a time we were... incredible together. You couldn't have forgotten it, Gar. I know I haven't. What harm could it do to have a glass of wine together?"

"Look, I'm sorry. I wish you well, and I mean that, but I just don't believe any kind of meeting is a good idea."

Ending the call—as he could have guessed—wasn't that easy. When he finally hung up, he glanced briefly at the still-cooling mug of coffee on his desk. Minutes before, he could have sworn he was desperate for a five-minute coffee break, but as always after talking with his ex-wife, he was edgier than a caged cougar.

He strode through Robb's office. "I'm going to make the rounds downstairs."

"You've got a couple more phone messages. Are you going to be back?"

"Yeah. Just give me twenty minutes. They were short in the kitchen before lunch, and there was a mix-up on a couple of reservations. I just want to be sure those fires are out. Page me if you need me."

"You want to be paged if she calls back?"

"Like I want a case of chicken pox," Gar said dryly. "But yes, page me for that, too."

The divorce was three years old, and the tie had

long been severed—until Janet suddenly started this calling. Continuing to say no to her made him feel coldhearted and cruel, but it had to stop. So far, nothing he'd said had stopped the calls worth beans.

He took the stairs down at a fast clip, but entered the lobby at a slower, assessing-for-problems pace. A fire roared in the fieldstone fireplace, making shadows dance on the arched beam ceiling of the main lobby lounge, where people were sprawled on couches and chairs, ski gear piled everywhere. Laughter rang out as the day's ski adventures were told—and embellished. Status quo for a late Friday afternoon.

Simpson was manning the front desk. Her first name was Bambi, but anyone who called her that—especially a man—risked his life. She had a wild mane of brunette hair and wore tight pants that showed off her fanny, but apart from that touchy women's lib thing about being called Bambi, she was efficient and cool with the toughest customers. Ralph was serving drinks by the fireplace—mulled wine, cocoa, spiced cider. He was a hard-core ski bum, but so far he'd proved reliable at the job.

Gar kept moving. Back in the kitchens, Jennifer was screaming like a shrew. Considering his cook carried 225 wrestling-weight pounds, one would have thought the kitchen staff might listen when she shrieked, but no. The crew all knew she was all bark, no bite, but she cooked like a man's fantasy. As long as Gar regularly showed up to exert some authority, the kitchen generally ran fine.

Although there were a couple of fresh fires to put out, generally all the spokes in the wheel were turning smoothly—and that was never a guarantee on a Friday. One of the waitresses caught his attention. Big pupils, hazy smile.

Making a mental note to check on the waitress again, Gar headed back toward his office. He took an occasional drink, but everyone on the staff knew he had a violent aversion to drugs—particularly the kind of recreational drugs that came with the fast-lane set. No one, except Robb, knew that his ex-wife was the source of that aversion. Her phone calls invariably reminded him of that old painful history.

He'd never known exactly when Janet first started substituting a glass of wine for something up her nose. He hadn't realized, because ambition was his god in those days, and working eighteen-hour days was his idea of fun. When she was under the influence, she'd strayed into other beds. And money had started disappearing like water.

Janet had always loved money. Hell, so had he. They'd lived high—no reason not to, he was rolling in it—and from the country estate to the sports cars she loved, Gar had happily indulged her. She'd been young and beautiful and he'd been crazy in love. She'd liked a party and she'd liked to entertain.

When he began to suspect who and what she was entertaining, it wasn't like he'd sat on it. He'd cared. He'd still loved her. And his own guilt had shot his conscience with a painful bullet. Maybe his workaholic ways had caused her loneliness, caused her to take that first dip into cocaine. He'd changed his ways, turned his life around trying to make things right.

But that hadn't stopped her lying. Nothing had seemed to stop Janet from lying at that point, and it was those lies that had eventually killed all feeling for her. He might have stayed in the marriage from responsibility, even then, but a counselor had helped him see that Janet's dependence on him was self-destructive. He couldn't rescue her—hell, he couldn't even get her to be honest with him. The divorce had jolted her into seeking professional help.

He'd come out of it battered. Positively the failed marriage had permanently tempered his love affair with ambition, and that had been when he sold his other business holdings and came to live in Tahoe. The lodge was work to run, but he'd learned to balance play and work. The healing process took longer. The experience with Janet hadn't soured him on women, but it had made him wary of his own judgment. And he had deep—justifiable—fears of entering any relationship where honesty between both people wasn't an absolute from the very start.

For a man who had never wanted more than a wife, children and a normal family, the mighty irony was how money had sabotaged him. He never had given a royal damn about it. It wasn't his fault the business deals he touched turned to gold. It was the challenge and bite of wheeling and dealing that tickled his fancy. The stash of green he kept accumulating was actually irrelevant to the process...but not to women.

Women were either drawn to it or worried about it. Either way, money always put up a barrier. He never again wanted to be involved with a woman where lying and subterfuge were a threat, but somehow his damned bank account muddied up the waters.

He strode back upstairs, past Robb's desk and into his own office, where his gaze lasered on the plate on the far corner of his credenza. It was Abby's plate, the cookie plate, and for days now he'd known he should return it.

But he just wasn't sure what he was getting into. He'd only mentioned business a couple of times with her. Both times, something stark and wary had flashed in her eyes. Maybe she had something against money, too? And more to the point, no matter how lethally enticing that kiss, no matter how damn fascinating he found the lady...she fibbed. And not eensy fibs, but whoppers. About her not crying, when she was bawling her eyes out. About her being the relaxed, laid-back type, when a damn fool could see she was a time bomb of energy. And he'd come to the obvious conclusion that seeing her again just wasn't the wisest of ideas—

"Mr. Cameron?"

He swung around. Only the brand-new employees called him Mr. Cameron; he just didn't run that kind of formal ship. Yet Susie had been with him for six months, and darned if he could figure out what the Sam Hill he was doing that still had her intimidated. She was one of his ski pros, and her freckled young face misleading; she was a gifted teacher, and incredible with novice kids on the slopes. "Problem?" he questioned.

"Yeah. There's a lady, hit a tree, knocked herself out." Susie twisted her hands, rushing nervously to explain. "She was a first-time beginner, shouldn't have been anywhere near the intermediate slopes—anyway, she's okay. She came to, we brought her in on a stretcher. Only she's really raising hell about seeing a doc."

Accidents came with the ski business—and so did

lawsuits. Gar had stiff rules about how his staff handled injuries. It was standard practice for a medic to check them out before the customer left the premises. "She's raising hell about wanting to see a doc, or not wanting to?"

"*Not* wanting to. She keeps saying she's perfectly fine—except for being embarrassed to death. But, Mr. Cameron—"

"Gar."

"Gar." Susie tried it, but Gar had the feeling they'd be back to "Mr. Cameron," no matter how many times he told her. "The thing is, she knocked herself out really good. And yes, she does seem okay. I don't think there's any threat of broken bones, but she *really* hit her head."

"Okay, I'll handle it. Where is she?"

"Down in First Aid. I hate to bother you—"

"Susie, that's exactly what I'm here for. You're never bothering me when you bring me a problem."

"Well, she keeps swearing she would never sue anyone and we're making a big fuss over nothing. But none of us think she should be driving. We're talking a real goose egg on her head. I think John should check her out for a concussion, but nobody can seem to get through to her."

"It's okay," Gar said again, and held the door open so she could scoot ahead of him. "You did just right."

They hiked down the hall and stairs together, but Susie was still knitting a sweater with those hands. "I just feel I should have handled this without having to bother you. I mean, it's really my job—"

"Some people just get their knickers in a twist, Susie. And those are the folks that are *my* job. You get a jerk, you're supposed to come to me. And a Friday night like this, I know we've talked about this before, there's always a risk of some partiers or drinkers on the slopes. If you see trouble coming, I want to know."

"Okay. And yeah, I know you've told me." Susie exhaled. Even came up with a smile.

By the time they rounded the corner into the first aid room, Gar wasn't sure what to expect. Usually it was a man who put Suzie in a tizzy, someone coming on too strong, and the poor kid was so hopelessly cute that some of those come-ons were inevitable. But women didn't throw her often, so Gar was guessing the lady in question had to be a pretty good witchy bitch.

Truthfully, he was about prepared for anything.

Except for what he found. Four of his employees were crowded in the small first aid room, all talking at once, in calming, soothing voices. He had to duck around them to catch a look at the slim, blue-jacketed figure sacked out on a stretcher.

Abby.

He remembered trying to talk her out of changing a flat tire in a blizzard. It was no wonder his employees couldn't get through. He'd already learned the hard way—arguing with Abby was like trying to reason with a blockheaded hound.

Chapter Four

"Clear out," Gar said to the crowd.

His tone was more mild than authoritative, but it still had the effect of waving a magician's wand. The bodies flooded out. The door closed. All the noise and confusion that was making Abby's head throb abruptly disappeared, but darn. Now she had a six-foot-three-inch headache to contend with.

This day hadn't gone at all the way she planned.

Abby swung her legs over the side of the stretcher cot. Unlike all his employees, Gar didn't attempt to stop her.

"I seem doomed," she said dryly. "If you had a bad first impression and a bad second impression, you'd think I could have counted on that old adage about the third time being a charm. Gar. I'm not hurt. I'm fine. I just want to go home. Where I can die of embarrassment in peace."

"Uh-huh."

He stepped closer. She saw his fisherman's sweater and the casual slacks and she had the impression he was studying her hard, but she didn't venture a look at his face to find out. She didn't want to meet his eyes, not while her stomach was still churning ominous threats that she could still be sick as a dog. "Your employees are all bullies," she informed him.

"Yeah, they're good, aren't they? They're supposed to get tough when someone's hurt."

"Well, beyond a couple of bruises, I couldn't be less hurt. And I don't have a concussion. And just for the record, I didn't hurt your tree."

"Ah. It was a tree that caused this, um, golf-ball-sized lump?"

"Ouch."

"Sorry." He didn't sound sorry. He didn't remove his hands from her head, either. "You sure there isn't a big hole in my tree? You know...I could have sworn I saw you on the beginners' slopes earlier this afternoon."

"Well, I started there," Abby grumbled. "But the novice hill looked so Mickey Mouse."

"How long have you been skiing?"

"Three hours."

"I meant, before today," he qualified.

"Three hours sum-total skiing experience, Cameron. And don't give me that look. It looked like so much fun, and I usually pick up things quickly, and I love speed—" She swallowed when he gently, firmly tilted her chin. He was studying her, all right. Relentlessly. Although heaven knew whether he was checking for dilated pupils or actually seeing *her*.

"And you couldn't stand turning down the challenge of the bigger hill?"

"No, no. I have no interest in challenge or competition. I told you, I'm the lazy, laid-back type—"

"Yeah, so you said." He let her go. Maybe it was accidental that he chose to lean back against the door, arms crossed loosely, miraculously blocking her exit. "I've got a deal for you. I won't drag you kicking and screaming to the emergency room, if you'll at least let John, our medic, take a look at that bump on your head—"

"Heavens, that isn't neces—"

"And in return for doing me that favor, you've got a room on the house tonight. Penthouse floor. Dinner brought in, no cooking, no dishes, free movies, balcony view—"

"For Pete's sake, I don't need to stay here!"

"For Pete's sake," he echoed, "I don't think you're up to driving. Your hands are shaking. You're white as paper. And you'd be going home to a place with no one around to call if you needed help."

"I—"

"You're going to have a hell of a headache, if you don't already. I'm guessing you're bruised up, as well. If you stayed here, all you'd have to do is pick up a phone and someone could be there lickety-split. Unless there's some reason you *have* to be home, it just makes logical sense to stay, doesn't it?"

"I..." Darn it, he was talking too fast, confusing her into believing this whole plan sounded reasonable.

No woman would trust that sudden slow, sneaky grin. "If you're thinking any strings come with the room.... Aw, hell, I admit the thought crossed my mind. But I have this rule, written in stone—no seducing women with goose eggs on their heads. Never broken that rule yet, so you're safe. Another time I hope to give you some real, serious trouble, mind you, but tonight I guarantee you have nothing to worry about—"

"Cameron," she said with an exasperated scowl, "I was not worried about that."

He waggled his brows. "Well, good. It's settled, then. We'll get you set up upstairs, have John check you up there, where you're comfortable, then you can wallow in a good hot bath. Afraid Friday's my busiest night, my beeper goes pretty nonstop, but I'll join you for a quick dinner around eight—if you want the company."

Abby could have sworn she said no to that entire program. His staff all clearly understood the word *no,* but with Gar, it was like trying to communicate in Swahili.

He was smoother than a con artist. Faster than greased lightning—which was bewilderingly fast—she found herself exiting the penthouse elevator, holding a brand-new toothbrush, escorted by a short, bearded man in a starched oxford shirt named Robb.

Robb unlocked the door to a long, rectangular room, paneled in pecan, with splashes of forest greens. On the left, the sitting area had an overstuffed green couch, big-screen TV, coffee table and desk. The bed, on the right, was big enough for a couple of orgies, and draped with a lush, plush forest green spread. Tiffany lamps flanked a stone fireplace in one corner, where a cheerful fire already spit and spiraled, scenting the room with hickory and pine. Doors led out to a balcony and a view of the ski slopes.

"Good grief, I don't need all this," Abby said desperately.

"Uh-huh." So far Robb's chief conversation had been limited to *uh-huhs*—except when he was delivering orders. He must have tutored under Gar, because he had a lot of those. "John, our medic, will be up in a minute, so maybe you don't want to get too settled in until you see him. Gar ordered a tray of tea and a snack to be sent up, should be here anytime, too. After that, nobody should bother you for a while—there's a bathrobe in the bathroom, phone in there, too, a menu for dinner, if you'll take a look at it..."

When he was gone, Abby dragged a hand through her hair, almost positive she'd never agreed to staying, much less to any of the rest of this.

It had seemed such a simple thing this morning. Coming here. Trying out a pair of skis. Pretty crazy to come to Tahoe in the winter and *not* try skiing. Taking up the sport was part of her ruthlessly determined agenda to learn to play, to turn over an entirely different personality leaf. And she hadn't chosen Gar's ski lodge with any intention of seeking him out, but if a chance meeting happened—all the better.

For three days, the embrace between them had festered in her mind like a toothache. Aggravating. Testy. Unignorable. The thing about alligators under the bed was that there was only way to make them go away—you had to crouch down and look and see for yourself that nothing was really there. *Should* she happen to run across Gar, Abby figured, she'd have the chance to face him in nice, normal circumstances. And all that silly chemistry she'd imagined in her mind would be put to bed.

But she'd never anticipated remeeting him after an embarrassing fiasco with a tree. She didn't just hurt. She seemed to have bruises where she hadn't even known she had body parts before.

Worse yet was realizing she felt battered from the inside out—and one look at him had still produced a blast of hormones. Her stomach had been queasy, for Pete's sake. And that strange, confounding chemistry was still there.

A sudden shiver laddered up her spine. Nerves. An uneasy restlessness. A sensation of fear, as if she had some premonition of danger. Foolishness, Abby knew. She wasn't afraid of Gar—or chemistry. Until she was fired, this strange exasperating feeling of vulnerability had never preyed on her. She'd just never felt lost before. In principle, she understood perfectly well that she'd taken a wrong road, and the solution to such a mistake was cut-and-dried. A strong woman didn't run from a problem. She faced it. She fixed it.

Only, tarnation. Abby was more than willing to face and fix—but she just couldn't seem to get a clear picture of what the right road was for her.

The arrival of John, Gar's medic, interrupted her troubled thoughts, and everything started to go better. John was a six-foot-four-inch RN with a gentle baritone and an even gentler sense of humor. After that, a tray of tea was delivered, chamomile, with some stomach-soothing crackers to go with it. She ended up taking a mug with her into the bathroom, and soaking in a warm, steamy bath for a good half hour. Once she dried off, she decided to curl up under the burrowing-warm green comforter for just a few minutes.

Two hours later, she woke up. Not being a nap taker, she was disoriented for a few seconds. Slowly, though, she swung her legs over the side of the bed and then pulled on her black pants and black-and-red angora sweater again.

She still had a headache and some aching bruises, but sleep had done its job and helped restore her equilibrium. She was starved, and as she prowled the room searching for her purse and hairbrush, she determined that she was more than up for blowing this luxurious pop stand and driving home.

Abruptly she heard knuckles rapping on the door, and a man's voice called out, "Room service."

Gar could easily see from the startled look on her face that she'd expected a room-service waiter, not the owner of the place. Taking advantage of her surprise—and the open door—he wheeled in the two-tiered cart, talking as he set it up by the coffee table.

"I didn't want to risk waking you up if you were sleeping, but I figured you'd need something to eat around now—and I did, too. Friday night's my killer, anything can happen and usually does. It'll take some real luck to get through dinner without an interruption, but in the meantime..."

In the meantime, he looked her over. A few hours before, her face had been the color of paste. Her cheeks were rosy again, and the shine was back in her eyes. With her arms cuffed around her chest, the bare feet and tousled hair, she looked as if she'd just been caught climbing out of bed—a tempting, enticing thought, if the bed was his—but Gar schooled himself to behave.

"I'll be damned. You look human again," he murmured. "I don't see any bruises, but I'm guessing more than a few must have shown up by now."

"Maybe I'm a little beat up, but I'm not giving myself any sympathy, so don't you, either. Women who tangle with trees deserve what they get." When he first walked in, Abby had wrapped those arms around herself awfully quickly—an instinctively wary gesture, Gar mused, and a natural one. She was unsure if she was being chased, unsure what she thought of him altogether as yet. Thankfully, however, the lady had more pressing priorities. Faster than a finger snap, that edgy wariness disappeared. Her eyes, in fact, were having a lust-fest—but, regretfully, not for him. "Food? You brought food?"

"Yup. Chicken soup for you. And a sixteen-ounce steak for me."

"All I get is *soup?* And you get steak? Are you aware your hero status is shooting straight down the drain?"

With a grin, Gar started dealing out silverware and dishes. "Sorry, brown eyes, but that's the way the cookie crumbles. I talked to John. He said light food only, just in case nothing heavier wants to settle on your stomach."

"My stomach is begging for a horse." She wasted no time hurling herself on the couch, within easy grabbing reach of all the mysterious covered dishes.

"John specifically said no horses." He settled thigh-bumping close—solely because it was easier serving her. "On the other hand, I got a bunch of unpleasant orders, too. John said I was supposed to feed you hand-to-mouth, not let you do a thing. I'm even supposed to butter your muffin, pour your milk—"

"Milk?"

"Yeah, that's all you get. Milk. Maybe when you get older, we'll let you graduate to a glass of wine or something with caffeine. But John said—"

"I spent twenty minutes with your medic, Cameron. John impressed me as a no-nonsense, practical, competent RN. There's no way he came up with any of this bully routine. You're feeding me straight malarkey."

Well, that was true, Gar mused. But malarkey was also working so well that he wasn't inclined to upgrade and behave. She'd easily and naturally relaxed with him...and he had an agenda with this dinner. His hormones were under the mistaken impression that getting his hands on Abby Stanford was the only thing that mattered. It had been a lot of years since he was exposed to chemistry with the volatility of a tornado. He liked that chemistry. Too damn much to feel easy with it.

Diving off the deep end wasn't his way, not unless he knew what he was getting into. She'd fibbed to him before. Since Janet, any woman who waltzed around the truth made him nervous. Abby had no reason to share any "heart truths" with him—hell, she barely knew him. But spending time with her was the only way Gar could get a sense of whether they could be, might be, honest with each other in a serious way. Before letting loose any more of that disastrous, tumultuous chemistry, he just needed to find out more about who she really was.

And he found out. "Hey," he growled.

Not a trace of guilt in those guileless brown eyes. None. "The soup is wonderful. Tasty. Real homemade noodles, and the chicken's unbearably tender...but your steak is better. Rare and raw."

"You're not supposed to have heavy food," he reminded her as she stole yet another forkful from his plate.

"I'm weak from my injuries. I need real food to build up my strength.... What's in your thermos?"

"Coffee, thick enough to be petrified. My favorite kind. No," he said firmly when her eyes lit up. "Caffeine really could make your headache worse. That's no lie."

"One sip? Honestly, my head's better. And are those covered dishes—dessert?" She didn't wait for an answer, just reached over and lifted the lids to take a peek. Under one covered dome, she found a bowl of big-pearl tapioca. Under *his* dessert dish, she discovered a marshmallow sundae with chocolate ice cream.

"You touch that, you die," he informed her.

"You'd hurt a wounded woman? A delicate flower who nearly killed herself on a traumatic fall from your ski slopes? Have you no sympathy? No compassion?"

He removed the sundae from her reach. "Chivalry's dead, Stanford. Live with it."

"My, my. A little possessive about our chocolate, aren't we?" With her eyes on his, shimmering with the honesty and sincerity of a Girl Scout, beneath his range of vision she grabbed the dish. "Honestly, I just want a teensy bite. You won't even miss it."

Teensy bite? "You're leveling it," he said accusingly.

"Not out of meanness," she said reassuringly. "It just occurs to me that you have an obvious 'in' with the kitchen staff. I think it's fairly likely you could have forty sundaes made up in the next hour if you really wanted them."

"That's not the point."

"Ah. What's the point?"

The way her pink tongue darted out to caress that spoon, he damn near forgot his own name, not to mention the thread of the conversation. "The point is that I thought you were a nice, decent woman. Instead, you're showing me your true colors. Selfishness. Greed. Ruthlessness."

"I can't tell you how much those sticks and stones wound," she assured him. "But I told you from the first, I'm into a lazy, decadent life-style. What you see is what you get. Have you got any more hidden food over there?"

She was already snuzzled pretty close to him, but when she leaned over to pilfer more goodies from his stash, he caught a whiff of peach shampoo and lemon soap...and her. The swelling and tightening in his groin was immediate. A teenage boy's response. Disgraceful in a grown man. Still, he'd have been happier if he could write off his physical response to the sexy, spicy scent and the nearness of her slim, lithe body with the excuse of deprived hormones.

His hormones had been deprived before. He'd survived. The nasty, pervasive charge he felt with her was coming from a more subversive level entirely.

It just wasn't possible to have this much fun with a woman he barely knew. They still hadn't shared a single meaningful word; he still didn't know one serious thing about her. But the damn woman was like sunshine, bright and warm and natural. He had to watch his take-charge ways with most women, but Abby gave back as good as she got. It was like one leaf recognizing another leaf from its home tree. She knew how to give nonsense back to one of her own kind.

"Well, it hurts to admit this," she murmured, "but I think I'm finally full. And it's all your fault I ate so much."

"*My* fault?"

"Totally. This whole thing started out by my being a dimwit and taking a tumble on your slopes. I'm not used to being rewarded for being a dimwit by being spoiled to death. Not that I'm not the spoiled, pampered type, mind you..."

He could see how pampered and self-indulgent she was. Two seconds after she finished—and claimed she was too stuffed to move—she quickly started stacking dishes instead of leaving them for the obviously paid staff to take care of them. For someone who made repeated claims of laziness, she had more energy than an Eveready battery. She was clearly about to spring from the couch when he grabbed her hand.

He didn't know exactly why he did it. It was just some instinct, some impulse. But the instant she felt his fingers thread with hers, she slowed down—way, way down. "Talk to me," he said quietly.

"I've been talking nonstop through dinner—"

"Yeah. I haven't had a dinner that was this much fun since I can remember. And I'm finding that... confounding. I like people, but I rarely feel comfortable with someone I don't know, and Abby, I don't know you at all. What do you do for a living? How do you happen to be in Tahoe?"

Her gaze met his squarely, but those eyes of hers had the depth of a dark lake, nothing on the surface, nothing he could read. Beyond nerves. She was suddenly, definitely, nervous. "At the moment, I'm doing nothing for a living. And plan to be in Tahoe for the next two months, specializing in doing absolutely nothing meaningful if I can possibly help it."

She was ready with that light, joking answer, but her eyes didn't reflect any of the devil-may-care lightness she claimed to own. Her face, her shoulders, her whole body, were suddenly tense. Gar was perplexed. A simple query about what she did was hardly a big prying question.

"You were unhappy with whatever work you were doing before?" he asked carefully.

"Yes. Exactly. Old history, nothing I want to talk about or go back to—so I'm just taking a big, long, lazy vacation to figure out what I want to do next."

"Any ideas on your mind?"

"*Anything* that's not related to business," she said curtly, and then squeezed her eyes closed. "Good grief, that came out wrong. I didn't mean to offend you—just because it's not my field doesn't mean I can't respect someone else loving it. It's obvious you have a terrific place going here, and that you have a real love and talent for management—"

"Well, when I first took over the lodge, it was a

pinch away from Chapter 11. It's come a long way, but it also has a long way to go. To be honest, the place picked up and started booming before I was really prepared."

"Problems?" she asked him.

"Hell, I never met a problem I didn't like...but yeah, there've been a ton." He offered more. "I started out from a little town in Georgia you've never heard of, then ambled into Atlanta, then Houston. This has become home, but I never really expected that would happen when I took on this failing child. I know business from the manufacturing side of the fence. I never had any background or knowledge about what it'd take to turn this type of place around."

Initially Gar had thought that if he offered more about himself, she'd feel more comfortable about opening up, too. Instead, she somehow circled any question about herself and aimed it back at him. For someone who'd leaped to express a distaste for business, she directed a steady, enthused stream of questions about the lodge and how it worked, both charming and challenging him with that endlessly quick mind of hers.

And then, from nowhere, her voice abruptly trailed off in the middle of some question. Why, he didn't know. Lodge management was hardly a fascinating subject, but for sure there was nothing troubling about it—and she'd been the one avidly pursuing it, bubbling away, all animated and excited...

Suddenly, though, there was silence between them. Nothing happening in the room beyond the spit and sizzle of fire in the corner grate, the jeweled glow of light from the Tiffany lamps...and the texture of her hand in his.

Gar couldn't remember the last time he'd held a woman's hand. Holding hands seemed to be something he'd left behind in adolescence and discovered bigger, more interesting and dangerous things. Like sex. Holding hands shouldn't make a man....ache.

Yet desire seeped through him like a treasure trail. Her fingers were small, slight, soft. No rings. His bigger hand could have swallowed hers, yet fingertips touched fingertips in a slow dance, touch and retreat, touch and retreat, like an echo of wooing foreplay. *Am I gonna let you any closer? Can I trust you? How far can I tease?*

The same shyness was in her eyes. She had to be near his age, and everything about Abby spoke of mature confidence and competence...yet there was a young girl in those eyes, unsure what was happening, unsure and a little afraid. He had the crazy impression that she'd never said hello to chemistry before, or, like him, couldn't believe this was happening from simply holding hands. Yet it was. A delight in each other. A simmering, shimmering desire, like a dare and a promise for the future.

Her palm suddenly cushioned his, making a natural nest of their hands. She pressed. He pressed back. Talking with their hands like damn-fool teenagers, Gar thought, but he didn't feel at all like a damn-fool teenager. He'd wanted this dinner together to understand her better. That mission seemed to be a total failure, yet somehow he'd stopped giving a royal hoot if he could understand or define anything.

He felt *right* with her.

Thirty-six years old. Once married, definitely battle-shy and guilt-scarred. But he could not, for either his mistakes or the good things he hoped he had credit for, remember feeling this sense of rightness. Not with any woman.

Still clasping her hands, he leaned closer. She knew the kiss was coming. Positively knew, because she leaned into him with lashes shadowing her cheeks in soft velvet spikes. Her lips parted, her breath no more than a drift of a whisper. And he'd almost claimed that kiss—and God knew where it would have taken either of them—when the sound of a staccato knock on the door startled both of them.

Gar stiffened instantly. Friday nights, he was never "off." Interruptions were as inevitable and predictable as rain. He couldn't believe that he'd forgotten that she had been hurt earlier, forgotten his lodge, forgotten that he had clear intentions of never laying a finger on her. He shot off the couch, expecting a business problem and trying to yank his head back to where it belonged.

Impatiently he pulled open the door, and immediately felt a porcupine ball of nerves roll in his stomach.

The brunette standing there was wrapped in fur, and she was clutching the full-length coat like a homeless—though well-made-up—waif. "Gar. The woman at the front desk said she'd call you up here, but then she got busy with something else for a minute, and, well...I wasn't sure you'd see me if they paged you. I understand you must be busy with something, but if I could just see you for a few minutes..."

Gar had been prepared for a problem with battling staff, a reservations glitch, a drunk in the bar, any and all kinds of disasters. But there was no way he had anticipated or was in any mood to handle his ex-wife.

Chapter Five

One look at the brunette put wings on Abby's heels. She snatched her purse and shoes, smiled, said something polite, and escaped from the scene somewhere between the speed of sound and the speed of light.

Down in the parking lot, she dived into her brass-cold Lexus and cranked the key. The engine sputtered unhappily. Her Lexus was usually an angel, and she positively didn't need a car with an attitude tonight.

She cranked the key again. The engine took off that time, and so did she, barreling out into the black-silk night, toward home. She reached over blindly and pushed buttons, lots of them—heat, defrost, fan, radio. Springsteen was crooning the old one about dancing in the dark. She turned the volume up so loud it made her head pound—but that was neither here nor there; her head was already pounding from the lump she'd gotten earlier. More to the point, Abby figured she deserved the headache. Hell's bells, what she really deserved was another whack upside the head.

Gar clearly hadn't expected the interruption by the fur-draped brunette, but even her existence underlined an obvious home truth for Abby—she knew very little about Garson Cameron. No thirty-six-year-old man—or woman—was fresh from the sandbox. Grown-ups came with a history, and to assume a man was unattached because he kissed her and had dinner with her was damned stupid. Abby wasn't used to behaving stupidly...and yes, she'd figured out that scene in the lodge room in two seconds flat.

Gar wasn't precisely attached, because the brunette had eventually identified herself as his ex-wife. The woman's appearance was still flashing in Abby's mind like a Kodak photo. Gorgeous hair. Beneath that fur, a dipping-low black dress, pricey, nothing vulgar or tasteless about it, but the fur alone had probably saved her from pneumonia. It wasn't covering much. The makeup was. Blush and foundation had skillfully covered all flaws—that was wildly assuming the woman had any—and what she wanted had been in her eyes.

She wanted Gar.

Abby's foot exuberantly leveled the accelerator. At this precise moment, she strongly guessed, the lady was doing her best to seduce him. Whatever the divorce had been about, the woman wasn't wearing come-to-bed perfume and dressed like that for a little chat. She wanted her ex-husband back.

That was a lot to deduce from a five-second exposure, yet Abby had seen what she'd seen, and really didn't doubt her intuition. There was just this sick, thick knot in her throat. Blaming Gar wasn't an issue. He'd never expected his ex-wife to suddenly appear, never asked for the awkward situation. But the strange, compelling closeness she'd felt with him seemed a measure of how goofed-up her whole thinking was lately. Naturally Gar had a history. How could he not? But she'd never gotten between a man and his unfinished history before, and didn't intend to now.

That was the stuff you were supposed to get straight *before* you kissed a man. And for damn sure before you started imagining wild, silly, foolish fantasies that had absolutely no basis in reality...

Abby clenched her jaw. And concentrated on driving. The road curled around like an abandoned shoestring, her Lexus hugging every curve. The bright lights of Tahoe's casinos and nightlife glowed in her rearview mirror, beckoning with their promise of noise, company, distraction.

She wouldn't mind a couple hours hiding from herself, but not tonight, when she felt too much like a welterweight who'd lost all ten rounds in the boxing ring. She needed sleep, peace, and a couple of aspirin. She reached the condo in record time. She had just unlocked the door and was just tossing down her purse and keys when she heard the phone ring.

She grabbed the receiver in the living room and, as soon as she heard her sister's voice, pushed off her boots and promptly curled up on the turquoise sofa. A call from Gwen couldn't have been more welcome. Gwen was the earth mother of the three sisters, always full of common sense and comfort, and a ton better than sleep, peace or aspirin any day of the week.

Except this time. Gwen had barely thanked her for

sending ten dozen cookies before she barreled in with "Listen, I couldn't seem to find an easy flight into Tahoe—not a fast one, anyway. But I checked, and I could get a flight landing in Reno tomorrow afternoon. That's close enough, simple to rent a car and drive to you in Tahoe, if you just give me directions—"

"Whoa." Abby flicked on a lamp switch and dragged a bewildered hand through her hair. "Make that a double whoa, sis. I haven't a clue what you're talking about—"

"Spense'll take care of the kids, so that's not a problem. And Paige wanted to come too, but honestly, while she's still nursing the baby it's really har—"

"Neither one of you need to come. What on earth even put this idea in your heads?"

"You did," Gwen said patiently. "I don't know what's wrong. Neither does Paige. But it's perfectly obvious to both of us that you're really unhappy—"

"Gwen. Back up. Relax. Put your feet up. I'm *fine.*"

"And elephants waltz. One minute you were thrilled with your job. The next minute you've taken off for Tahoe at the drop of a hat, as if your life and job in L.A. never existed. I'd be delighted that you were doing something impulsive, except that you don't have an impulsive bone in your entire body. Something is obviously terribly wrong, and since you refuse to talk to either of us on the phone—"

"I'll talk. I'll talk." God. Sisters. You could fool a boss, a lover, and for damn sure a mother, but never a sister—at least not one of hers. Abby washed a hand over her face. It never seemed to matter how much they argued and bickered, how completely opposite they were in personalities. They'd always had an unshakable bond of love from the heart. She had a bad feeling her sisters would kill for her if they had to.

God knew, she would for them.

"I told you both about the promotion I didn't get, losing my job." Abby wrapped her arms around a couch cushion. "Maybe it bothered me just a little bit more than I let on."

"You want Paige and me to hire a hit man for the turkey who fired you? Offhand, I'm not sure where you go about hiring people like that, but believe me, if—"

"That's all I need. Contending with your two adorable husbands blaming me because you two were in jail."

"We can handle our husbands," Gwen said darkly. "Let's get back to the problem at hand—namely you—and unless you immediately start talking about how you're feeling and what the holy horsefeathers you're doing in Tahoe..."

"Hey, I told you I'd talk." But Abby closed her eyes, not wanting to go into this, not now, not tonight, not even with Gwen. "I just need some time. Time to...change. And I didn't pick Tahoe for any special reason, except that it was a place where I could get totally away from everything about my life in L.A."

"Okay. Go on. What about this 'big change' you want to do?"

"I don't know, exactly." Abby hesitated. "I just realized how much I made business my whole life. Everything. What I wore, where I lived, even my choice in car and how I decorated my apartment—every stupid breath I took was about my career. And

I *loved* my work. I never saw anything wrong with what I was doing...until I lost the job, and it felt like the whole rug was swept out from underneath me."

"Oh, Abby. Paige and I told you a zillion times that your career was wonderful, but it mattered too much to you. You never even let a man get close."

"Hey. I like that whole half of the human species. I never had a problem getting along with the guys. I *like* men, for Pete's sake."

"Didn't say you didn't. I said you never let a man get close. I don't know what you're scared of...."

Blast her sister. Even after Abby hung up the phone, she sat scowling at the dark, cold, empty hearth. Her sister had it all wrong. She wasn't scared. Of anything.

But she'd never been an earth mother the way Gwen was. And Paige was an artist; there was a feminine sensuality in everything about her. Both her sisters had seemed to find women's roles that fit them as naturally as old, comfortable gloves. Abby never had. She recognized her own set of talents, but they had always made her a lone wolf. She was a competitive achiever—like men. A go-getter and a lover of battles—like men. She'd always secretly felt that she was a faker and a fraud at this woman business. She'd just never been good at....well, *girl* stuff.

Slowly she climbed off the couch and headed for bed, pep-talking herself up every stair. Maybe the self-criticism wasn't strictly fair. The truth was, she'd never *tried* girl stuff. Now was the first time in her adult life she'd ever had free time, and two months dipped ahead of her to experiment, to find a new balance in her life. To find out, when it came to the crunch, who she was as a woman.

Being fired had left her feeling fragile and vulnerable, Abby knew. But there had to be some woman's role in the nineties, some niche for her. All she needed to rebuild her confidence again was to succeed at something, to *not* fail.

When the lights were out and she was snuggled in bed, her mind spun back to Gar. No matter how much she enjoyed being with him, no matter how winsome and sexy and inexplicably drawn she felt when she was with him...he was a dynamic, successful man, and at least temporarily, her life was in downright shambles. In the best of times, she'd never been good with men on a personal, intimate level. And with painful honesty, Abby realized that allowing a relationship to develop any further with him was just asking for failure.

She had to stay away from him. There simply was no other choice.

Gar was leaning against his Cherokee when her Lexus zipped into the drive the next afternoon. Abby obviously spotted him, but she was wearing dark shades against the glare of winter sunlight, and he couldn't see her expression. He'd been waiting at her place for a full half hour. The cold didn't bother him, but he was as fidgety as a claustrophobic in a submarine.

"Hello," she called out when she opened the door. Nothing else, and there was nothing in her voice to help him guess if she objected to finding him here. She stepped out of the car, but then bent right back in to grab some packages. Her arms started filling up with bags.

He jogged forward to help when he realized how much she was trying to carry in. "You buy out the stores?" he asked.

"Well, I got just a little overenthusiastic. Needlepoint and candlewick and crewel..." He must have looked blank, because she chuckled and filled him in. "Girl stuff. Crafts."

"You like crafts, huh?"

"Me? Heavens, yes. I'm a craft lover from way back."

Her tone was oddly firm, as if she thought he might doubt her. There was nothing to doubt. She was balancing enough crinkly, crunkly packages to block her face, sabotage her walk to the door, and for sure make it difficult to ferret out the house key from her purse. "I never did see a point in doing anything halfway," she said with a laugh. "Although I did seem to overdo it just a teensy bit this time."

As far as he could tell, she was gonna be doing crafts until the year 2025. On the other hand, he *had* noticed her teensy tendency to do everything 200%, from her flat-tire battle to her cookie making to her first experience on skis. The tenacious thought had lodged in his mind that she'd love that way, too. Go for it. No holds barred and screw the risks. For anyone or anything that really mattered to her.

Not that Gar had any wild ideas that that "anyone" could be him. But the awkward debacle with his exwife the night before had itched on his conscience like an allergy. Somehow, something had gone wrong every time they were together, either her disasters or his. Hers he couldn't fix. But his he sure as hell wanted a chance to explain.

"Abby—"

"Just set the bags down in the living room, okay? I'll bring in some coffee. I left the pot on from lunch, so it's probably like sludge now, but I remember you saying—"

"Yeah. No such thing as too strong for me. Sludge is my favorite flavor."

There was no chance to talk with her for several minutes, not while she was flying around at jet speeds, what Abby seemed to call her relaxed pace. He juggled the packages and carted them into the living room. When that was done, he stood restlessly, not ready to sit, but not wanting to be caught pacing, either. The couches were a striking turquoise color, but everything else was wood and stone and glass. It was a man's room, with big furniture, lots of space, and the view from her French doors was a canal for a backyard—iced over now—leading to the blue-green waters of Lake Tahoe.

"Here you go...afraid it *is* sludge, but at least it's raspberry-almond sludge."

He whirled around to take the black glass mug from her. She was still breathless from running around, but her jacket and boots were gone now. She was wearing pale yellow slacks and a matching oversize angora sweater that swallowed her torso. The color and texture made her look soft, vulnerable, fragile. Crushable, Gar thought, and took a breath.

"I wanted to explain about my ex-wife—"

She was shaking her head before the words were even out. "You don't have to explain anything, Gar. It's not my business. It was really obvious that meeting was awkward for you. I didn't duck out to be rude, but just to get out of your way."

"Yeah, it was awkward. But I'd still appreciate the chance to explain—it had to look like Janet was a regular visitor or still a part of my life. We were divorced three years ago."

"Okay."

She curled up in a corner of the sofa, but she clearly wasn't going to ask any questions, much less invite any confidences. Gar took a gulp of coffee, and decided that being beaten up in a back alley by a gang of thugs had to be more fun than this. "Janet got the idea about a month ago that she wanted to see me again. I don't know why. We occasionally communicated over business or financial matters left over from the divorce, but she never called or pushed like this before—and last night was the first time she ever just showed up, uninvited. Her place is in Houston. She has some old friends in Reno, and often used to spend a weekend there, but I had no reason to know she was anywhere near Tahoe."

"Really, you don't have to tell me any of thi—"

By his code of honor, he did. "I don't kiss one woman if I'm still attached to another, Stanford. I'm not attached. Legally, emotionally, or in any other way," he said bluntly.

"I… Okay."

Well, nothing particularly seemed "okay." He threw himself into one of the overstuffed turquoise chairs, thinking that honesty was really a rotten policy. It'd be a lot easier to shut up. But he didn't. "After you left, she came on to me," he said flatly.

"Um, I hate to break this to you, Gar, but a nun

could have figured out she had that in mind,'' Abby murmured wryly.

''Well, damned if I was expecting it.'' He clawed a hand through his hair. ''Look, I'm not having any fun telling you about any of this...but I want to see you again. And I can't swear that my ex-wife won't call or do something else that...well, that looks wrong.'' Since he seemed to be wallowing in mud all on his own, he figured he might as well dive for the bottom of the puddle. ''I have a hard time being unkind to her, Abby. She got into cocaine when we were married. Deep. Destroyed about everything in her path, including our marriage, and definitely including her.''

Abby's expression had been almost unreadably cool and calm, but suddenly there was heart in her eyes. ''Oh, Gar. I'm sorry.''

''I was a workaholic in those years. Hardly home. Busy building an empire, inhaling every challenge, happy as hell. While she was sinking lower than a stone.''

''You blame yourself,'' Abby said gently. She didn't waste breath phrasing the comment as a question.

''I didn't see it. Didn't see her loneliness, didn't see how much trouble she was in, didn't have any comprehension of how well she'd learned to lie to cover up the problem. I don't know if you've ever encountered anyone on drugs—''

''They were everywhere in Los Angeles. The corporate world no different than the ghetto.'' She sighed. ''Growing up, I had the naive idea that good people never fell off that cliff, but nothing could be less true. Anyone can get suckered in."

"Yeah. Exactly. But I'd never been around it, had no concept of how the drug would change her whole personality. She turned into a complete stranger, nothing like the woman I married—but the point was...she couldn't climb out on her own. I don't blame myself for starting her on the habit. But maybe if I'd been less self-centered, less a workaholic, I'd have realized it earlier, confronted her while she still had some control over it—"

Abby shook her head fiercely, protectively. "You must know by now that it doesn't work that way. Talk to anyone who's been on drugs. Talk to any therapist who works with them. There's only one person who can rescue someone with the problem—and that's the person themselves."

"Yeah. I know the 'talk.' In fact, I was counseled into getting the divorce when I did.... On the surface, it has to look cold-blooded to desert someone in trouble like that—"

"No, it doesn't," Abby said quietly.

"Well, it did to me. But her doc told me damn bluntly that the best thing I could do for her was get out. The thing was, she could get money from me, find ways to hide the habit, knew I'd keep bailing her out... It wasn't like she still felt love, but just this unhealthy dependency on me. And basically that seemed to prove true, because she checked into a rehab center as soon as the tie was severed. As far as I knew, she'd straightened out her act, was doing okay. With the divorce she got the Houston house and property, and a lump sum for alimony—which was exactly what she asked for. I never argued, never bickered about the amount, nothing like that. The point being, when this was done, there were no hanging threads, no reason to still be in contact with her."

"Until she started calling again? And you're thinking she may show up in black slink and furs another time?"

"Nothing happened, Abby," he said quietly, "and nothing was going to happen. She startled me, and I wasn't real happy with the way I handled it. There wasn't any question about her staying with me—in any way. But I've told her no before, and I sure as hell must be doing it wrong, because nothing's gotten through to her so far."

Abby cupped her chin in a palm. "I think there's a lot of rescuer in you, Cameron," she said softly. "You stop to help damn fool women with flat tires. You pamper idiots who collide with your trees. I'm afraid the evidence was pretty damning, even before you told me about Janet. I don't think you'd find it easy to be cruel, not to a woman."

Gar wasn't sure what to say. He'd expected about anything but warmth and sympathy.

She smiled suddenly. Just a slight curve of her lips that put a spring-softness in her eyes. "You're really miserable talking about this, aren't you?"

"I've had more fun at an IRS audit."

She chuckled. "Well then, we're done with this. Put it to bed in your mind. If she happens to show up when I'm around again, I'll know what's going on. Wish I had some great advice to suggest on how to handle her, but I honestly don't have a clue. I think when something's this hard, you just do the best you can and try not to beat yourself up about it."

Again his throat went dry. "You don't have to be this understanding. I just need you to believe that I'm being honest with you."

"I believe you."

"You're not ticked?" He still couldn't believe it.

"You think I should be ticked? Because we were embroiled in a pretty tight clinch when a beautifully—and nominally clad—brunette walked in with the clear intention of seducing you?" She was chuckling, teasing him, when suddenly the oddest shadow seemed to darken her eyes. "Cripes, I guess a normal woman would respond by being ticked, huh? I don't know what's wrong with me. I could try getting mad or hurt or something—"

"Uh, no. That's okay," he said with dry, wry speed.

"I just kept thinking how awkward and miserable I'd have felt if someone had walked in like that on *me.* I'd have died. A couple of times over. You think I should have been angry?"

The conversation had taken a mighty humorous turn. Gar had the craziest feeling she was going to talk herself into *getting* ticked, if he wasn't damned careful. "I think I owe you—I think we owe each other—at least one time together when there isn't a disaster going on."

"They do seem to follow us," Abby admitted.

"So how about a dinner?"

She hesitated, and he thought, Damn. She hadn't hesitated once since he walked in, not about listening to him, not about openly offering him understanding and empathy. But it seemed to just now occur to her what direction he was leading in. Time together.

She curled a leg under her, pulled at an earring, shifted a couch pillow, all the while looking at him, studying his face as if she could find answers there. He'd have given her answers, if he'd known the questions.

"Gar," she said finally, "I'm...uneasy."

"Over sharing some prime rib and a baked potato?"

She chuckled. "No. Of course not. But..." Her voice softened, sobered. "I'm in the middle of a bunch of life changes. Nothing terrible, just some choices and decisions I have to make, and I'm really not sure where I'm going to be two months from now. If you want some company, someone to talk to or just be with...I'm fine with that. But I think right now I'd be a pretty bad risk if you were looking for more than that."

Gar stood up and grabbed his jacket. Definitely time to leave while he was ahead. Just occasionally Abby seemed to think like a blonde. She didn't, for instance, seem to notice that he was the one who'd established himself as a bad risk, because of his whole past history with Janet. She'd just seemed to accept that mountain. He couldn't imagine another woman who would.

"If you were afraid I was going to pop an instant marriage proposal...rest easy. I was, mind you. I was going to forget all the common sense and life experience I've accumulated up to age thirty-six, and blindly leap right into a committed relationship. But then I remembered your stealing my chocolate sundae."

She grinned. "You're gonna hold that against me *forever?*"

"Let's just say I think fellow chocoholics have an excellent basis for understanding each other...and it seems to me we've both earned some play time. Which means—in part—that we're not going anywhere for dinner that doesn't have a range of chocolate desserts."

"Not your lodge. You'll never get any feet-up rest time there."

"You've got that right. Tahoe, thankfully, has a full-service nightlife. And I happen to know where they serve the best chocolate." He zipped up, then aimed for the door. "Seven o'clock suit you?"

"Sounds great."

"You want to do it jeans or dress-up?"

"Dress-up."

"Where was my head? In Tahiti? I knew it was a mistake to ask a woman that question," Gar muttered humorously. "It'll probably take me until seven to scare up a tie. If I have to go to all the trouble of dressing up, I'm warning you now to get in a nap, because I'm not promising to get you home before dawn."

She was just starting to sputter, something about "Men!" and "Why do they ask you a question if they don't want to hear an answer?" when he leaned over and dropped a kiss—on her nose.

Silenced her completely. Seconds later, he was outside and hiking for his Cherokee, whistling, the sudden cold stinging his cheeks, thinking her response to that smack on the nose had been damn fascinating.

So was she. Increasingly fascinating to him. Her

warmth, her perception, her humor. That incredibly pugnacious chin. The mystery and depth in those gorgeous dark eyes. She turned on, flushed like an innocent schoolgirl, for a smack on the nose. Abby should know damn well it was dangerous to give a man an ego stroke like that. She could make a guy believe he was something special—or could be special to her.

Gar peeled out of the driveway with sun blinding his eyes, and his ebullient mood suddenly sobered. He wanted to be blinded by Abby. He couldn't remember, ever, being this captured or captivated by a woman. He wanted those compelling feelings...wanted her... wanted to believe they had the potential to go somewhere powerful and real together.

He was damned afraid that he was falling in love with her.

Yet his instinctive male antenna warned him against rushing into risking his heart. Abby was obviously deeply troubled by some problem, something that had led her to hiding out in Tahoe. He told himself it was unreasonable to expect her to open up when they'd known each other such a short while. Trust took time.

Still, her tiny fibs and evasions troubled him. He'd had one marriage irreparably crippled because of a lack of honesty. It was a mistake he wouldn't, couldn't, make again. And there would come a point, Gar knew, when they would have nothing unless Abby took the risk—and was honest with him.

Chapter Six

He hadn't kissed her.

Abby glanced at the living room wall clock, but it was barely after one. Way too soon to leave for her ski lesson at two with Gar. She bent her head, and stabbed the needle into the needlepoint canvas again.

Her mind had been replaying her date with him two nights ago like an incessant broken record. They'd started the evening at the top floor of Harrah's, where the food was splendiferous and the restaurant's atmosphere luxurious and intimately private. They'd bumped hips at a roulette table in the casino for a while after that. And danced after that. He'd brought her home, maybe by four, and hovered in her dark doorway for another twenty minutes, talking. Through the whole evening, speaking conservatively, he'd probably had four thousand, three hundred and twenty-seven opportunities to make a pass. But he hadn't kissed her.

Even once.

Abby pulled up the yarn and discovered a knot in it. Scowling, she flipped over the needlepoint canvas to see if she could find the problem. Normally she loved challenges, but this was on a par with isolating a single drop of water in the ocean. The canvas backing already had an uncountable number of knots and gaping bits of yarn.

The thing was...she'd been dressed in red silk that night. Nothing flaunty, but the dress clung where it was supposed to. She'd carefully chosen perfume, makeup, heels to show off her legs. If her appearance hadn't attracted him when she was in that get up, nothing less than a complete body transplant was likely to work. Positively Abby was unsure if she even wanted the friendship to dive into sexual waters, but tarnation—why hadn't he kissed her?

Frowning darker than a thundercloud, she sprang from the chair and yanked the needlepoint canvas over to the window light. The living room was already littered with other craft projects she'd started—like the crewel picture, and the cross-stitch bell pull, and the candlewick pillow. Theoretically, none of them were hard to learn. You pushed a needle in. You pushed it out. You made knots. That was it. Cripes, women had been doing—and loving—this stuff since the beginning of time.

Why couldn't she?

How come she seemed to fail at everything that any normal woman could probably do in her sleep?

Impatiently she glanced at the wall clock again.

Thank heavens—time had slipped away while she was having all this fun. The knots in the needlepoint would have to wait. With all this messing around, she needed to make fast tracks to meet Gar on time.

She'd only casually mentioned giving skiing another try...but Gar had gotten this humorous look of alarm, and dryly suggested that—for once—he'd like to save his competition any injury lawsuits. If she really wanted a lesson, she could come to the lodge and bypass all his extremely qualified instructors; he'd teach her himself.

As if for some reason he thought she wouldn't listen to anyone else.

It was a disturbing thought, that Gar had already come to know her so well, but she had no time to dwell on it. Burrowing into a jacket and boots, she hit the door at a fast jog.

Outside, the sun was blinding-bright, but it was still cold enough to make her breath smoke. On the drive there, she glanced at the rearview mirror and realized she'd forgotten lipstick. And a hairbrush. Not that appearance issues mattered, she thought glumly. By the time Gar saw her, her nose'd be a windburn red and her hair squished down under a hat, and ski pants always had made her thighs look like tree trunks. There wasn't a prayer of her looking remotely attractive.

For the dozenth time, she warned herself that she shouldn't be *wanting* to attract him. She had never leaped into an affair, and she didn't want to now. It was just...everything seemed different with Gar. He made her laugh; he was impossibly easy to be with. His loneliness touched her own, and the way he talked about his ex-wife had shown his integrity, his honesty, his heart. And yeah, hormones were a factor, too. Kisses had been different with him. The performance terrors and insecurities that always, always, hit when she was alone with a man...she just didn't seem to remember them. Not when Gar touched her.

She *felt* sexy with him. Feminine, sexy, even a little...wild. Free like she never felt free. And her mind kept shooting her that secret word, *maybe.*

Maybe.

Abby turned into the Cameron Crest parking lot with her pulse racing like a jet engine. She'd never had nerves or anxiety like this. She had to get those "maybes" out of her mind. His ex-wife had failed him big-time. Gar didn't need another woman who didn't have her life in order and her head on straight. The risk of failing him was the risk of hurting him.

She'd never been good at this woman business. Take a simple needlework project that started out looking like flowers, and her flowers somehow ended up looking like sick fish.

Maybe Gar sensed it. Maybe he somehow sensed that at the core, she was a failure at the woman things that mattered. Maybe that was why he hadn't kissed her the other night.

Abby climbed out of the car and jammed her stocking cap on. *Quit thinking like that, you dimwit. Just... quit thinking.* She squared her shoulders and glued on her most cheerful smile. They were gonna ski for a couple of hours. They were gonna have fun. There was absolutely nothing at stake in this little outing—except spending a few hours getting laid-back and relaxed, and playing. It was exactly what she was determined to learn how to do. And she was going to lick this fear-of-failure thing—or die trying.

Heaven knew what was wrong, but Gar figured it had to be pretty terrible. Threat of bankruptcy? A dog that had died? Food poisoning?

He'd never seen such a fake, hearty smile. There were serious nerves in Abby's eyes, and she was far too edgy and restless to even try standing still. Gar considered kissing her—as both a diagnosis and a treatment. The idea was tempting. Just swoop her up, yank her arms around his neck, level a good one on her...and see where it took them. Maybe she'd talk to him then. She'd told him volumes the last time he kissed her—in fact, he judiciously considered that that was a fine way to get honesty out of Abby, without either of them having to say a single word.

Momentarily, though, a satin-white ski slope stretched in front of them. And the kind of kisses he had in mind were far better suited to a private atmosphere. Skiers milled all around them. Gar hunkered down and clipped the binding on her ski boot at the heel and toe. "How does that feel?"

"Feels great. Is that it? Are we ready?"

"Can't wait to try out that slope, huh?"

"You bet."

Uh-huh. He stood up, ignoring all the strangers crowding around as if they didn't exist, and concentrated solely on Abby. He'd supervised all her equipment choices, and although Ms. Speed Lover didn't know it, that had included applying a certain wax to her ski runners that would help slow her down. Even so, she was bound to wipe out if she didn't shake some of that rigid stress and loosen up. *Limber* didn't seem to be in her vocabulary today. "Do a couple of knee bends, okay? Clomp around a little. Let's see how the skis feel for you."

"Okay, gotcha."

He watched her do about ten knee bends—in a second and a half. She clomped a foot away, then a foot back, then looked up at him expectantly. She was *ready.* Gar scratched his chin. This was a little like coaxing a high-strung Thoroughbred to chill out at a racetrack. "We should probably start out with a short lesson on theory. There are four types of downhill skiing."

"Yeah? What?"

"First, you have downhill racing. The idea is just to get from point A to point B in the fastest period of time."

"Okay."

"Then there's slalom racing. Instead of aiming in a straight line, you zigzag on a slalom course. And the giant slalom type of downhill skiing is another form of that—basically the difference is the length and scale of the course. Then the last type is the super giant slalom, which is a combination of regular downhill and the giant slalom, and involves long high-speed turns, that kind of thing...."

"Okay. Which are we gonna do?" she said impatiently.

"Our goals," he said gravely, "are much more complex." With one arm on her shoulder, he motioned with his other toward the whipped-cream slope rolling below them. "You're going to try to get from up here...to down there...without killing yourself. That's it. Now, do you remember how to stop?"

"Of course, I—"

"Show me." She endured that, then unwillingly endured another lecture on slowing-down techniques. She memorized lingo and theory well, he gave her that. But whether she was actually listening, Gar didn't have a clue. "You see those trees?"

"Now don't start rubbing that in, Cameron."

"I was just trying to point out that they're really a long, long way from the course. In fact, the whole purpose of keeping that line of pines was to establish a nice, clean, big space between the separate ski runs. We've never had anyone collide with those trees. Before. I mean, unless you work really hard at aiming completely off course, it's honestly pretty hard to ski anywhere near—"

He saw the gloveful of fresh, fluffy snow coming at his face—but not in time to duck it. The wayward temptation to kiss her again was damn near irresistible. She started chuckling when he hammed-up wiping off the faceful of snow. Teasing her was obviously the key to making her relax. For a minute.

In the next minute—perhaps she feared retribution, or another ponderous lecture—she was gone. Knees bent, fanny aimed at him, ski poles angled just like a pro, she took off with a whoosh from the hilltop.

Gar poled off fast just behind her, sticking a protective distance just off to her side. Snow smoked behind their skis. The day was priceless, three inches of fresh powder, no wind, a pale sun adding brilliance and beauty...and halfway down the run, he caught the joyful peal of her breathless laughter. Real laughter.

The speed was exhilarating her, which he could have guessed, but watching her shed that stress and anxiety was a satisfaction for Gar as nothing had been in a long time.

At the bottom, of course, she forgot how to stop. He saw her skis turn, the runners cross. He whipped next to her, but not in time to save her a spill. She crashed on her fanny, skis aiming in the air like tangled stilts, but she was still chortling with laughter.

"You okay?"

"Are you kidding me? I can't wait to do it again!"

Normal beginners tired after a few up and downs. Their new muscles protested. And the cold naturally got to them. Not her. Five runs up the gondola and she still wasn't worn down—or daunted by any number of exuberant spills.

"Well, you think I'm ready for the advanced run yet?" she demanded.

"You may be ready, but you're stuck with a wimp in this twosome. You know how long we've been doing this? Do the words *thirst* and *starvation* mean anything to you?"

"Oh." She glanced around. "I see you have lights on the slopes."

"The lights come on," he mentioned tactfully, "when dusk falls. And as fast as you've taken this on, toots, I don't think we're going to let you ski at night until you've had just a little more experience."

"I'll bet it's beautiful at night."

"It is." To distract her from that line of thinking, he added plaintively, "I need feeding."

She looked him up and down with a critical eye, and a cheeky feminine grin. "Well, you are looking a little hollow, big guy. And I suppose I owe you, after stealing your entire afternoon."

"You do." Gar couldn't think of a single reason to let her off that hook.

"And I suppose if we eat here, at the lodge, you'd just be interrupted a million times."

"You've got that right." Just in case the option hadn't occurred to her, he slipped it in. "You could always take me home."

She burst out laughing. "I wouldn't try taking that pitiful routine on the stage, Cameron. There's just something about you that totally fails to look helpless. But all right, even knowing I'm being suckered, you've got me feeling sorry for you now. I'll take you home and give you a home-cooked meal."

Rather than have Abby stuck driving him back to the lodge later, Gar followed behind her in his Cherokee. He'd barely stepped in her place before he started inhaling—in a few short days she'd turned a bachelor pad into a woman's haven of smells, vanilla, peach, sandalwood, jasmine. And her living room was unrecognizable for the yarn and scissors and patterns and kits all over the place.

"Man, you weren't kidding about loving crafts, were you?"

"It'll clean up, it'll clean up." In one circular run, she swooped up all the debris from all the spare surfaces, dumped them behind the couch and then grinned. "My theory on housekeeping is, out of sight, out of mind."

"I can see that."

"Even a woman into hard-core girl stuff can't do everything. Housekeeping's where I draw the line. On the other hand, I can whip up dinner in just a few minutes...."

Gar wasn't sure what she planned on "whipping up," but she scrabbled up a written recipe from an envelope in the kitchen, and out came ingredients. The recipe was for lasagna, he thought, but the pans and pots and bowls kept mounting up. He wouldn't have staked his life on it, but she seemed to be making enough for a dinner party of twenty.

"You can put your feet up, if you're tired," she assured him.

"I'm the one who's used to skiing. You're supposed to be the tired one. But you'll have to give me a couple of clues here. I don't know how to help unless you give me a job."

"You sure? With you living right at the lodge, I wouldn't think you'd have many chances to learn how to cook—"

"I had a life before-lodge. And Janet wasn't into cooking, especially in the last couple years..." He didn't want to get back into that subject. "Trust me, I can cope in a kitchen. You want me to open some wine? And I can put together a mean salad."

Underneath her ski gear, she wore a soft black sweater over white leggings. Neither fit tight, just temptingly snug enough to make a man obsess on wondering what was beneath them. That was, of course, assuming a man could ever catch up with her in order to find out.

As he shredded lettuce, he watched her fly around the kitchen, preparing a feast for the marines. She kept zealously checking her recipe, but she also looked outright bewildered at the amount of noodles that plumped up. She looked even more bewildered at the overflowing pans. But she never mentioned food. She was into talking business. His business. A subject that Gar would have sworn she'd claimed to seriously dislike.

"You know, I noticed you had people of all ages on the slopes," she mentioned.

"Yeah, like I told you, the lodge was a long way from solvent a few years ago. But especially this season, it's taken off in leaps and bounds. Grown faster than I expected or was prepared for," he admitted.

"I also noticed that you also had all kinds of groups—singles, kids, serious skiers, hobbyists—sometimes bumping into each other. Have you considered anything like a public relations or specific advertising program?"

"I've more than thought about it. I know it's needed, just haven't had the manpower or time to really pursue it. In the beginning, I was running pretty hard, just getting the place on its feet. And now is really the time when some serious planning could make a difference that way."

She nodded thoughtfully. "You're not as big as Heavenly or Squaw Valley. But that isn't a problem, it's just a dimension that needs to be considered. You need to make your smaller size an advantage."

"Advantage?"

"Yeah. You know. You need...an identity. To establish that you're not competition for the big kahunas—nor trying to be—but a place with its own ambience. So first you need to define the nature of the customers that you really want, and then develop a program that will specifically attract those people."

By then, Gar had finished uncorking a burgundy and was tipping the bottle to top off her glass. Candles were lit on the black glass table, the lasagna bubbling, the salad long done. Both of them were in stocking feet, and as far as he could tell, Abby was relaxed, animated and full of life—until she suddenly stopped talking and an odd, stricken look filled her eyes.

"What's wrong?"

"I've been talking business with you for almost two hours, for Pete's sake."

"Yeah, and I love your ideas. They're terrific." It occurred to him that this wasn't the first time Abby had strayed into business waters. After she claimed such an antipathy toward business, Gar had first assumed she was just being polite, asking about his work. But something was off kilter and untrue in that picture. Her perception of his management problems was right on target, her understanding something a layman should never have had. Somewhere she must have picked up serious experience in some business field, no matter what she'd told him...and confusing him even more was her obvious exuberance and enthusiasm the whole time she'd been talking.

Yet now she dragged a hand through her hair with a troubled expression, as if the whole subject were some source of guilt. "I like cooking. And crafts," she said firmly.

Well, she sure persisted in claiming to. They'd been doing fine, Gar thought, talking as easily as old friends, having fun with the whole conversation. Until something upset her, something that seemed to have to do with business. Cautiously, he tried opening that door again. "Look, if you have the free time, I'd love to have you come to the lodge, brainstorm some of those ideas with Robb there, too—"

"Oh, I couldn't, Gar. Heavens, I was just shooting the bull—"

"Nothing you said was bull. You were talking about the exact kind of public relations program I'd like to put together, but just haven't had the time—or the manpower—to get something started. Abby, if you misunderstood— I would never ask you to do anything like that without paying you."

"Money has nothing to do with it."

"Well, it would to me. At some point I'd have to hire someone to put together a PR program for me, anyway. The kind of ideas you brought up are exactly what I expect to pay for. Just think about it, okay? I understand you're on vacation, but if you get bored...even if you just wanted to come in and toss some concepts around for a couple hours—"

"No, really, I just...can't."

She whirled around and served dinner. Gar couldn't remember a time he'd wanted to give a lady a whomp upside the head, but he could see her slumped shoulders, see those soft lips compressed tighter than a sealed envelope. "Can't" was an entirely different response from "don't want to."

He never actually meant to press her—hell, he could find someone to do his advertising and PR. But her eyes had been shining like beacons when she was pouring out those ideas. She'd expressed such perception of his management problems that her familiarity and expertise were clear. She'd obviously done this type of work before. She obviously loved it.

So why did she keep denying the truth?

It bothered him. From the beginning, Gar had suspected that something was troubling her. He'd guessed a man. And he could well understand wanting to keep certain kinds of secrets. Why should she trust him? Yet he couldn't fathom any possible risk in her being straight with him about loving business—or not loving cooking. Why tell fibs that didn't need telling?

She was beautiful. He loved her full-of-hell humor, loved that swift, sassy mind of hers. Loved watching that fanny swishing around at top speed, her courage barreling into anything new, that pugnacious chin. But dammit, he was scared of liars. He had reason to be. Although the source of his ex-wife's lying had been drugs, his marriage had become a living hell because there had been no way to honestly address or face any problem.

"You don't like it." Abby sent him a worried look when he swallowed the first forkful of lasagna.

"Are you kidding? It's out of this world."

She dived in too, then. "It's my sister's recipe. Gwen's. She's an incredible cook..." She glanced at the voluminously filled pans. "But I must have forgotten how much the recipe made. She's always cooking for an army of kids."

"You're really close with your sisters?"

"Thick as thieves. The three of us are total opposites in personality, but it never seemed to matter. You have brothers and sisters?"

"One older brother. Left the nest long before me, but there were legions of Cameron cousins to fill in the blanks. Family's a big deal to us, too."

Abby mounded salad on his plate. "I'm guessing a stranger walking into one of our family get-togethers would be pretty terrorized. It's noisy, and we argue, and we talk nonstop because we don't get to see each other very often."

"Sounds like ours. And my clan's nosy besides. I swear, there's no one in my family who ever heard of the constitutional right of privacy. They've got prying down to a well-honed skill," Gar said dryly.

Her eyes started dancing again. "Mine, too. I'm the oldest of the three sisters. Growing up, some poor guy'd try to walk me to the door, I'd have two sisters' faces pressed to the window to see if he kissed me good-night. Darn near impossible for a girl to get in any interesting trouble with such unshakable watch-dogs in-house."

Gar could hardly let that go. "And were you, um, trying to get in trouble?"

"In theory." Her tone was droll. "I had a lot of big romantic theories when I was in high school. But reality was that I was probably as repressed as you could get. Had a terrible case of good-girl-itis."

"Good-girl-itis?"

"Uh-huh. Everyone else was drinking at parties, and getting tickets and fender-bumpers, and sneaking out from their parents' to sleep with their guys. I was home studying." She shook her head mournfully. "I was never even grounded, for heaven's sakes. What kind of life was that?"

He started laughing. "It couldn't have been that bad—"

"It was. Honestly, it was. And I swear, if I had to do it all over, I'd throw out the rule book and kick up my heels. Being too good, too serious, is a dangerous thing. All I knew was work."

"Now, come on. No guys in that whole picture?"

Possibly, Gar thought, it was accidental that she never got around to answering that question. They'd both leveled dinner quickly, because they were mutually starved, and Abby had doubtless been maxed out trying to sit still for a whole half hour. Actually, he had the same problem with overabundant energy. The instant they finished, she was up and at the dishes—so he up and helped. Cleanup only took a few minutes, and then she disappeared into the downstairs bathroom.

Since she'd taken that one, Gar went in search of another bathroom upstairs. The room was easy enough to find, but he really blinked when he switched on the light. As he washed his hands, his gaze took in the square lapis lazuli tub, the Jacuzzi, the phone and the piped-in stereo. Her rented condo definitely had its share of creature comforts.

As he strode back down the hall, he hesitated at the top of the stairs. Her bedroom door was open. He never actually meant to look. The light wasn't even on. But the bedroom had French doors leading onto a balcony, where moonlight flooded in, and his eyes snagged on the curious glowing shape of some strange object over by those doors.

It was that strange object that captured his attention, but it was impossible not to notice the rest. He stood there, rubbing the back of his neck, thinking that Don Juan could have decorated the room—the one mirrored wall, the platform bed big enough for an orgy, the thick, furry bedspread. Maybe sensual was sensual, but somehow this was a man's brand of blunt, in-your-face sexuality, rather than the subtle softness Gar associated with Abby.

He wondered if she knew what she was getting into when she rented the place.

He wondered what she dreamed of when she slept in that big bed.

And his gaze lanced again on the strange glowing shape on the dresser top across the room. It seemed to be a sculpture. Black and white—like ebony and pearl. The sculpture showed a woman's profile, her face tilted up, and it was her expression that riveted Gar. She was more than beautiful. She almost looked alive, her face reflecting such an inner serenity and vibrant joy in life....

It was Abby, he realized suddenly. Someone had done a sculpture that exactly captured—

"Oops." Abby abruptly came up behind him.

Chapter Seven

Gar couldn't remember the last time he'd been embarrassed. "Well, hell, you caught me—but honestly, I didn't mean to poke my nose in your bedroom. I was just walking toward the stairs, and I caught a glimpse of that sculpture on the far dresser. I was just curious—"

With a chuckle, Abby switched on the bedroom light. "You don't have to make an excuse for being accidentally nosy. The first time I walked in this room, I almost had a heart attack. I don't know whether the pilot who owns the place is a throwback to the playboy era—or a wannabe. Either way, his decorating taste lacks a certain, um, subtlety. And as far as the sculpture..."

She swiftly fetched the piece from the bureau and carried it back so he could have a closer look. "I can't remember if I told you that my youngest sister is a cameo maker. Paige made this one for my birthday out of onyx and pearl. I'm so proud of her that I about can't stand it, she's just so incredibly talented."

"You're not kidding." The sculpture had drawn Gar's eye from the shadows, but in real light the piece was even more breathtaking. "I thought cameos were jewelry. Like necklaces and earrings and stuff."

"Paige does jewelry work, too, but she's also sculpted free-form pieces of all sizes. It depends on the raw material she's working with."

"The woman in the profile looks just like you."

Abby chuckled. "I like the compliment—she's really pretty, isn't she?—but I'm afraid it's not true. There's no likeness. Paige has told us a zillion times that there can't be. She has this saying about sculpting work…that every piece of raw material has some kind of 'truth,' and the artist's job is just to carve away what isn't the truth. But the artist has no power to put something in the raw material that isn't there to begin with." Her fingertip stroked the soft, smooth profile of the woman. "I think it was no accident she chose to do this in onyx and pearl, though. Stark black and white. Paige says I've always been the all-or-nothing type. No grays. No middle ground. Or that's the way I *used* to be."

She was chattering pretty nonstop, but the comment about truth plunked in Gar's mind and gnawed on him.

The more he was with Abby, the less he understood who she really was. She claimed to love baking and cooking, when her unfamiliarity with a kitchen would have been obvious to a two-year-old. She claimed to hate business, and yet charged up anywhere near a discussion of it. And the single-swinger decor of the bedroom clearly embarrassed her—for sure, there was no in-your-face sexuality about Abby—yet she seemed unaware of the sensuality she did express.

It was subtle with her. Every truth that mattered seemed hidden under the surface with Abby. She had a full-of-hell smile, but she wasn't a hellion. Her eyes could brim with merciless sass, but deeper, darker emotions could flash from the depth of those eyes, too. She was tired now—and sure as hell should be, after skiing all afternoon—but even when she was in a bulky ski sweater, padding around in stocking feet, her shoulders never lost their proud straightness. For someone built so slightly, she had yet to show him the slightest fear of anything.

Yet she *was* afraid. That was always the reason people lied. The purpose didn't have to be as exotic as his ex-wife's trying to hide her drug habit, but shovel past any fib and there it was. Something the person was afraid of exposing.

Gar didn't know what the problem was. But he realized at that moment that the clues had always been there. Abby was afraid. Of something.

As quickly as she'd volunteered to show him the cameo, she carted it back to its place on the tall ebony dresser, hiked back toward him and flicked off the overhead light again. "If you already saw the bathroom, there's nothing else to see upstairs. There's one other bedroom, but it's locked up. I gather my landlord pilot stashes his personal things in there. Some of the ways he set up the condo really have me curious what kind of character he is—but I'm not complaining. He sure didn't short the place of luxuries. The stereo—"

One might have gotten the feeling from the speed of her nonstop chatter that she wanted him out of that bedroom. Now. Quickly. Yet, amazingly, she quit talking altogether the instant his fingers closed around her wrist.

Her eyes shot to his. As she stood in the doorway, her face reminded him of the black-and-white cameo, catching the light from the hall on one side, the shadows of the bedroom on the other. He lifted her right wrist to his shoulder. Then her left wrist to his opposite shoulder.

"I...I was going to tell you something about the piped-in stereo system...."

"So tell me," he said, encouragingly.

But she seemed to forget that thought altogether. She didn't move her hands. They rested around the curve of his neck, exactly where he'd put them. But she seemed to have sudden difficulty breathing, and those dark-almond velvet eyes hadn't left his for a second. "I... There's a balcony off the French doors. You can catch a peek of Lake Tahoe—"

"That's nice."

"You wouldn't, um, like to take a look?"

"I've seen Tahoe before. I think it's possibly the most beautiful lake on the planet. But no, I don't have any interest in looking at the lake right now."

"It's really a breathtaking view by moonlight—"

"Abby."

"What?"

"The more nervous you get, the more you're turning me on. If that's not the effect you want, you'd probably be a lot safer if you quit talking."

"I'm not nervous. I'm *never* nervous. And I'm not worried about handling you, big guy."

"Good," he murmured. "Handle me, then."

She almost laughed...but she didn't. Seconds spun. Soft, slow, silken webs of seconds, in which she obviously expected him to kiss her.

Gar wasn't positive why he waited. It wasn't as if he knew her so well. He had some intuition that she was short on patience—and incapable of sitting on a dare. She took on a tire in a blizzard. She ignored the novice ski slopes and went right for the gusto of the challenge. And he'd seen how she took on cookie making. Charge in. Full speed ahead. Inhale everything about a new experience in a single gulp.

But she hadn't volunteered to kiss him before. And when she made this small sound and surged up on tiptoe, Gar only had a second to brace. Her mouth collided on his with all the delicacy of a bullet. She communicated impatience, frustration and an inexplicable innocence with that spanking, flat smack.

Later it would occur to him that Abby had enough natural initiative to run a couple of small countries single-handed...but not in this. It shook her up to take initiative in this. And when Abby was wary or afraid of anything, take-the-bull-by-the-horns aggression covered it up so no one would ever know.

It was an interesting way to lie. And undoubtedly a very effective technique, if one was trying to endure a root canal.

But a lousy way to kiss.

His shoulder blades found a nice, hard wall to balance against. He drew her closer, pulling her into the vee of his thighs. Angling his head, he used his tongue as a paintbrush on her parted lips, moistening then. Tickling them. Painting them with his flavor, until she was enticed to taste a little more. And when her mouth opened farther, he plunged inside.

If he wanted truth, that was all he had to do to get it. This was Abby. The Abby that didn't show beyond that glossy, sassy, confident exterior, and the inside lady was a real different model. Soft lips drank him in, tasting of winsome shyness and a keening vulnerability. Her eyes closed as if she were shutting out the rest of the world. Her arms tightened around him, fingers clenching around his neck, as if she were lost and afraid of letting him go.

Her unsureness moved him as nothing else could have. Blood rushed to his groin. He'd never felt wanted like she made him feel wanted. Like he mattered. Like it scared her, because she wasn't prepared or expecting to feel anything this powerful.

Neither was Gar. He never played anymore. Ever. The emotional wear and tear cost too damn much if there wasn't a chance of something real and serious happening...and he *wasn't* sure of that with Abby. He wasn't sure of anything, except that no woman had ever felt this compellingly right in his arms. The risks would have to take care of themselves. He didn't give a damn.

Kisses trailed from her mouth, teased a rough-soft path down the line of her jaw. Hands tugged at her bulky black sweater, seeking her skin, seeking her. The need to touch her, really touch her, clawed at him like a cougar of desire.

She wasn't helping him keep that cougar leashed. Her arms shot up, making it easy for him to yank the sweater up and over her head. He spun her into the dark privacy of the bedroom, away from the harshly lit hall. Her skin was hot under that wool. A pale bra gleamed like satin in the moonlit shadows. But he'd barely dropped the sweater before she reached for him again, slim white fingers burying in his hair, pulling his head down for another kiss.

He slowed down.

Or he tried to. Those first kisses were soft, simmering, whisper-slow. And those first caresses were careful, reverent, respectful of that fragile ivory skin and her soft mouth. He didn't want to scare her, didn't want to rush her, and at some instinctive masculine level he understood that Abby was never as sure of anything as she let on.

But she responded with such dynamite. Impatiently tugging at his sweater, fretfully pulling it off him. Then coming back for another kiss, shivering now, the pulse in her throat beating restless and wild, her breathing coming and catching in a tearing rush.

He slipped the bra straps down her shoulders, trapping her arms, inciting a warm, wet wash of kisses down her collarbone, the delectable curve of her shoulder. Her fingers clutched and kneaded. He heard a broken sigh. An angry sigh. She wanted more.

He half lifted her to the bed. Then came for her. Their difference in height made standing awkward, a problem that wonderfully disappeared when they were lying together. The only slight repercussion was that he was losing his mind.

Moonlight flowed through the French doors, creating square patterns of light on her pearl skin. The scratchy fake-fur spread was black as midnight compared to her. Everything was black as midnight compared to her. Music kept building in his head, inspired by her responsiveness, the song of yearning in her eyes, the drumbeat of her need in her pulse, the rich, dark refrain of wanting building as her hunger escalated. And his.

He released her from the annoying scrap of a bra. Her breasts spilled free, softer than pearls, and she whispered a fierce moan when he washed the swollen tips with his tongue. Unsure what would please her more, he tried a tender suckling and then a nip, tried a fingertip caress and then a rougher kneading. He wasn't through with the evaluation. Maybe his control was tipping the scales toward dicey, but her feedback was so intimately, exquisitely responsive that he was considering extending the entire testing process for a couple more weeks—at least in theory.

Abby, it seemed, had a different theory. She suddenly twisted on top of him with a fury of a groan, her golden hair tousled as if from the wind, sweeping in his way, in her way. He was already harder than rock. If she was counting on him for sanity, he'd have had the same luck handling lightning. And she sparked more lightning, mercilessly, wickedly, by rubbing against him.

He'd have burned the white slacks off her, if that might have removed them faster. There had to be an opening somewhere. He couldn't find it. An exploring mission located the button and zipper on the side, but by then she was kissing him, her hands framing his face, not seeming the least interested in his frustration with stripping off the rest of her clothes.

A telephone suddenly jangled—so close, so loud,

that there had to be a receiver somewhere in the shadowed room. It was hardly an alien sound, but a gunshot couldn't have startled Gar more. Until that instant there'd been no one on the whole planet, as far as he knew, but Abby and him.

"I don't care," Abby said fiercely.

The phone jangled again.

She touched his cheek, looking at him, only at him. "Gar, I don't care. They can call back. Forget it."

But the caller showed no inclination to forget it, because the phone kept ringing. His head was swimming with magic—her magic—and he sure as hell didn't want to surface. But the phone was an intrusion of civilized reality, and with it came the buckshot sting of common sense. He had protection. Somewhere. But he was a grown man, for God's sake, and nothing should have gone this far before he either took care of protecting her or asked her. Nothing had been settled between them, nothing asked.

He groped for the bedside lamp, and nearly knocked it over before finding the switch. She blinked hard at the sudden bright glare in her eyes. The telephone rang again while he looked around the room, still unsure where the receiver was. The whole decor of the bedroom bulleted more guilt his way. It was another man's seducing lair, and it made Gar think of cheap, fast sex. A one-night-stand orgy haven. Nothing like what he felt for Abby. Nothing like what he wanted her to feel.

"Gar—"

Her voice was stressed and thready, but by then he'd spotted the phone on the dresser. He reached up and lifted both the receiver and cords over his body toward Abby. Whoever was calling her in the middle of the night was obviously expecting her and not a strange man, so he never considered answering it—but he heard the voice on the other end. It was a woman's voice, a lilting alto full of laughter, and she started talking even before the receiver was tucked against Abby's ear.

"I was just about to hang up. Figured you must be gone somewhere, Abby. But I had to call and find out, how'd my recipe for the lasagna go?"

The next afternoon, Abby zoomed in the parking lot of Gar's ski lodge. She cut the engine, grabbed her purse, the car keys and a dog-eared notebook, and climbed out of her Lexus with a scowl. The gloomy gray skies matched her mood perfectly.

She'd called Gar earlier in the morning to set up this meeting—but she hadn't wanted to. She'd rather suffer a case of chicken pox than face him this soon after the mortifying debacle last night had turned into. And there was no chance on earth she ever planned or wanted to become embroiled in a public relations program for him, or anything else to do with his business.

Gwen's phone call the night before had set this whole blasted awkward mess in motion.

Firmly she squared her shoulders, set her jaw and crossed the snowy parking lot at a determined clip. If her sister hadn't called at precisely the wrong moment the night before...but that, of course, was the problem. She *had* called. Abby cherished her relationship with her sisters. Unlike anyone else on earth, one could count on a sister to be there, to support you through thick and thin, to cover for you, to tell you straight if a dress looked awful...and, for damn sure, to interrupt the *one* time in your entire life when you didn't want to be interrupted.

The conversation with her sister had been innocent enough...until Abby suddenly caught her reflection in the mirrored wall of that playboy-wannabe bedroom—half-naked, her hair rumpled, her mouth red and wet. The reflection staring back at her had resembled a distinctly hot tamale, instead of the repressed, just-maybe-frigid cool cookie she'd always been.

Abby had never been swept away by a man, for Pete's sake. The whole idea made her feminist bones tch-tch.

Maybe—secretly—she'd been scared for years that she was always going to be that frigid cool cookie. A performance test-taker. A failure in bed. A woman who was going to have to be skilled at faking it, because that was all that was ever going to happen.

But, holy cow, she hadn't even brought up birth control with Gar. She'd acted like an irresponsible teenager instead of a grown, mature woman; that wanton reflection in the mirror had totally unsettled her...and she'd clutched up in a babbling, bubbling anxiety attack.

It wasn't the first time in her life she'd handled something badly. But this was *really* badly, and she'd telephoned Gar in the morning because she had to. An apology was required. Only, when she tried to explain, Gar somehow misunderstood. He acted as if the mortifying part of the evening had never happened, just leaped to the conclusion that she was apologizing and changing her mind about something else—namely her willingness to come and brainstorm about public relation for the lodge. It was so crazy—that wasn't what she'd been trying to explain at all. Gar had rattled her. Until she'd somehow agreed to come.

A crowd of skiers fresh from the slopes, juggling skis and equipment, blocked the entrance to the lodge. She ducked around them and headed inside. Under her jacket, she was wearing jeans and a red turtleneck—a far cry from the power suits she used to wear, but then, she'd sworn off dressing for success ever again. She'd also sworn never to have another thing to do with the business world ever again, but— Damn the man.

She knew precisely how he'd talked her into this meeting. He'd said he honestly needed some help. That was it. The whole sales pitch. And if that wasn't an ugly, low-down, manipulative way to twist a woman's heart, Abby didn't know what was.

How was she supposed to say no if he needed her?

"Gar is expecting me," she told the young woman with the wild mane of brunette hair at the front desk. Her name tag read Simpson. "I'm Abby—"

"Abby Stanford, yeah, I know..." The receptionist had troweled-on makeup and a wild hairstyle, but she was swift and efficient. "I was expecting you. Gar's up with Robb in the back meeting room.... If you take the stairs to the second floor, it's the last door on the left."

"Thanks."

Climbing the back stairs, Abby considered all the lions she'd confronted in a dozen boardroom dens, how much she'd always loved the adrenaline rush of a competitive battle. She knew the guys had called her tough behind her back.

She was feeling so tough right now that her hands were damp and her stomach was pitching acid. She poked her head in the doorway and there was Gar, slumped lazily in a winged leather chair, his long corduroy-encased legs stretched out...until he saw her. Another bucket of acid pitched in her stomach as he lurched to his feet and smiled, instantly, easily—a warm, intimate smile that made her knees want to turn into butter.

It wasn't right. It was terribly unright to lead a man on and then abruptly call it off with shaking hands and no better explanation than a bumbling "Sorry Charlie, I guess I'm just not ready for this." It *couldn't* be okay with Gar that she'd acted like a panicked goose. But he acted as if it were. There was no kiss—not in front of the other man right there. But he took her jacket, cuffing her neck for an instant at the same time, the gesture a caress, gentle, possessive.

"I could have guessed you'd be right on time.... Have you met Robb before?"

She recognized Robb from the day of her skiing debacle, but this was a different kind of meeting. The younger man was buttoned down and tied, his conservative clothes an incongruous contrast to his big, bushy black beard. His eyes, though, were as shrewd and sharp as lasers. Robb extended a hand before she could. She recognized an adversary from the brusque, clipped handshake, and relaxed some. Adversaries she knew what to do with.

It was only tall, dark giants with intimately warm smiles that knocked her for a loop.

"I'm glad you're joining us," Robb said cordially.

Sure he was. And cats flew. Abby set her notebook

and bag on the chair next to her, noting the oval table, the oak paneling and the oversize comfortable chairs. The casual setup seemed more typical of Gar's management style than any formal conference room, but they'd barely settled in before the telephone rang. Robb grabbed it and immediately exchanged a glance with Gar.

"It's for you, but I can handle it if you want," Robb said cryptically.

Gar rubbed a hand over his face. "No. I'll take it in my office upstairs. I'm sorry, Abby, but I'll take care of this as fast as I can. How about if you two pour yourselves a fresh mug of coffee—I'm glad you're going to get a few minutes to get to know Robb."

Abby guessed the call was from his ex-wife. Nothing was said, but the way the men looked at each other seemed a giveaway clue. She also guessed from the exchange that Robb was more than willing to protect his boss from lions, tigers, ex-wives...and upstart blondes in skinny jeans who he sure as hell didn't trust to have influence over his boss.

"I've been trying to get Gar to put a public relations program on the table for months," he said conversationally, as he poured her coffee from a decanter on the table. "Somehow you managed to do it, but he never mentioned anything about your background...."

Abby had been grilled by the best. He was good—but young. She was willing to oblige him, regardless. "I grew up in Vermont, but after college I interviewed for a number of jobs, and ended up working for a firm that had an opening in Los Angeles."

"Wouldn't think you'd get many skiing opportunities in L.A.," Robb said teasingly, but Abby heard the inference. What on earth did she know about ski lodges?

"I never skied in my life before last week," she admitted frankly.

"And is your home base still Los Angeles?"

Her mind flashed to the apartment on Hilliard Street—the closets filled with power suits, the walls decorated with the work of up-and-coming artists, every decorating item in the place chosen to fit the life-style of an upwardly mobile business exec. It was a place she'd once thought was perfect for her. Now she vaguely realized she had probably left some milk spoiling in the fridge. Unfinished business—too much like her life. To Robb, she said, "I still have a lease on an apartment there for the next three months, so I guess you could say it's still my home base—but that's temporary. Sometime over the next few weeks, I'll be making a trip back there to close it up and look for something else."

"So...you're changing jobs? What was your field?"

His tone was cordially sociable, but Abby figured this game of twenty questions wasn't really getting them anywhere. She opened her purse, pulled out her wallet and opened it for him. "You know it's a real driver's license picture, because I look half-dead," she said lightly. "But the vital statistics are all there. Blond. Brown-eyed. A hundred and twenty-two pounds. Organ donor. You can run a check with the cops if you want. No outstanding warrants. Honestly, I'm not out to hurt your boss...and have no interest at all in stepping on your toes in any way."

Robb sank back in his chair and scratched that woolly beard of his. "Did I, um, come across a little heavy-handed?"

"Nope," Abby said gently. "You came across as caring about Gar...which is all I need to like you. I understand perfectly well why you're reserving judgment about me."

"He's had a few women give him a run for his money."

A lot easier for both of them, once he put some straight cards on the table. She nodded. "And you feel protective, because he's a friend, as well as your boss. As far as I'm concerned, that's great—and if you're worried I'll take offense if you're suspicious of me, put your feet up and rest easy. Why the Sam Hill should you trust me? You don't know me from Adam."

"Dammit. I was positive I wasn't going to get along with you." The chill in Robb's eyes unthawed into a wry, crinkle-eyed grin. Still, he hadn't loosened up completely. "It's pretty hard not to notice you ducked every question I asked about your background."

"Yeah, I know I did. For a reason. I don't belong here," she said quietly. "I'm probably wasting your time and Gar's by poking my nose where it shouldn't be. But if it's any comfort—I promise I won't be here long."

She could see renewed curiosity in Robb's eyes, and swiftly she fired some questions at him about the lodge to divert any further personal conversation.

A lead weight of anxiety dragged at the back of her mind, though. Gar still didn't know she had any background in business. She had, in fact, billed herself as a traditional woman, heavily into cookie making and crafts, with no career interests anywhere in sight.

Abby had never intended to lie. But to confess to an extremely successful man that she'd been fired… there was just no way she could make the words come out. Her failure still ached like a raw sore. She'd felt so lost since the firing. So frightened. So painfully aware that she'd clearly taken the wrong road…and she just wasn't sure how to get to the right one.

And with Gar, somehow, from the very beginning, she'd felt like someone else. Feminine. Soft. Sexy. He didn't *know* she was competitive and ambitious and had all that nasty masculine drive. And she didn't want him to know. He was the first man, the only man, with whom she'd felt like nothing more—and nothing less—than a woman. Just a woman.

And it felt damned wonderful, until she clutched up and recognized the risks. Before, she'd failed a job. But she hadn't failed herself. She'd never been good at this woman business, and believing she could mean something to Gar had to be the craziest, wildest risk she'd ever taken. At the vast age of thirty-four, she'd never lost her heart before.

Abby had never been afraid of owning up to her mistakes. But there were things a woman simply couldn't fail at and be the same. Wherever this relationship was going—she didn't want to fail Gar.

Chapter Eight

The last thing Gar wanted to do was desert Abby for long, but the phone call from his ex-wife took more time than he expected. Janet claimed she was struggling with her drug habit, and that seeing him was the only way she could resolve issues that were inhibiting her recovery. He didn't want to argue with her. He didn't want to callously cut her off. But he'd heard all those sound bites from Janet before. His ex-wife was excellent with words, and she had a manipulative gift for coloring the truth to shift responsibility on anyone who'd take it.

He hustled back down the hall, rubbing the back of his neck. The sticky phone call had left him feeling as sharp-edged and wrung out as all the others, and he'd never meant to leave Abby alone with Robb for this long. As he rounded the corner into the conference room, though, he stopped short. His hand dropped back from the back of his neck.

Neither Abby nor Robb initially noticed that he'd walked in. No surprise. They were going at it nose-to-nose, talking ten for a dozen, noisily interrupting each other and squared off an exuberant verbal battle.

"No, no, no. That's a common mistake in advertising, knocking a competitor. Forget them entirely," Abby shot at Robb.

"The competitors are already the big names that everyone knows. They're the reference point that any skier would recognize—"

"But that's not how it works. When you advertise the negative, that's what people remember—the negative. You'll get further, faster, if you attack a problem from a positive angle. Give the lodge an image, an identity, that focuses on the clientele you want to have—and then go for it. Aim for what you want, not for what you *don't* want—"

"You're talking about a lot of money," Robb snapped.

"I'm talking about *effective* money. Dollars spent that will provably do a job for you..."

Gar doubted he could get in a word in—and for a few minutes, he was more than content to just watch. Robb was his right hand, the best administrator he'd ever had, but Robb was distinctly a paper person, rather than a people person. He didn't lack tact. He just never unbent. But his assistant, right now, had a tie hanging askew, a shirt untucked, and seemed to have thrown himself into a chair in a totally relaxed slouch for this...battle.

And Abby. God. Her face was flushed, her eyes

The Silhouette Reader Service™—Here's how it works:

Accepting free books places you under no obligation to buy anything. You may keep the books and gift and return the shipping statement marked "cancel." If you do not cancel, about a month later we'll send you 6 additional novels and bill you just $3.34 each plus 25¢ delivery per book and applicable sales tax, if any.* That's the complete price—and compared to cover prices of $3.99 each—quite a bargain! You may cancel any time, but if you choose to continue, every month we'll send you 6 more books, which you may either purchase at the discount price...or return to us and cancel your subscription.

*Terms and prices subject to change without notice. Sales tax applicable in N.Y.

were full of fire, her hair was ruffled up as if she'd yanked a hand through it a half-dozen times. She was wriggling all over that chair, charged up as if someone had lit the fuse on her personal dynamite. A kid at Christmas couldn't look much happier.

This from a lady who had had to be bribed, conned and cajoled into coming here. The lady who claimed to have no experience in or liking for business in any way.

Gar cleared his throat. "I hate to interrupt this..."

Both heads swiveled in his direction, as if they'd been interrupted by an unwanted gunshot.

"...but I'm afraid Abby has to leave."

"I do?" Abby said blankly.

"Uh-huh." Swiftly Gar gathered up her jacket and gloves. "She has something she has to do this afternoon. But I was thinking... Robb? We could move a desk in that side office downstairs. Abby's on vacation, but if she could spare us a few mornings to help with this PR thing, it'd be easier for her if she had an organized space to land."

"I'll take care of it." Robb grabbed a pad of paper and punched his ballpoint, and was already starting to make lists and muttering about computer terminals as Gar steered her out the door.

"Wait a minute, Gar...." Abby didn't seem to mind the hand under her elbow, leading her down the hall and up a flight of stairs. She never asked where they were going. She seemed suddenly so flustered she could barely get a coherent word out. "I don't... I didn't... I know I said I'd come in, but that was only because you asked for my help this one time. There's no reason for you to set up a desk—"

"Did I tell you about my cousin Ryder?"

She gave him another look of total confusion, as if doubly bewildered about how or why the conversation had shifted from desks to cousins.

"I told you I had a couple hundred cousins, didn't I?" Gar opened the door at the top of stairs, and subtly herded her left. "Well, Ryder lives in Colorado. Silver Springs. Just starting up a new business, doesn't have a clue how to promote or advertise. He's got a great concept going, but he just doesn't have any basic ideas for how to get it off the ground."

"Um, Cameron?" She waved a hand in front of his face, as if hoping someone sane was home behind those cool blue eyes. "I'm having a lot of trouble following this conversation. Are you telling me about your cousin for some reason?"

He grinned. And piled her jacket and gloves and scarf back in her arms, so he'd have a hand free to fish out the key to his suite. "Yeah, there's a reason. Ryder inherited a good slug of money. More than enough to pay you—and well. But he's damn young. Can't tell a fool from someone who's giving him good advice. I was thinking that you might not mind talking with him."

"I swear there's a piston short in your engine. You're not making a lick of sense. I never did understand why you wanted me to come in and brainstorm with you and Robb. And I can't imagine why you'd think I could help your cousin. I've told you several times that business just isn't my cuppa—"

"Uh-huh. I know what you told me. I also watched you level Robb, toots. Hell, I can't even level Robb, and he's been working for me for seven years. Handling my little cousin would be a game of tiddlywinks for you. He's smart, I swear, damn near brilliant, but he just doesn't have the age or experience to know what he's doing."

"Gar, I haven't given you one reason to think I know a balance sheet from a banana."

Yeah, she had. And Gar was beginning to pick up tattletale clues when Abby was trying to fib, particularly big fibs. Her eyes got this stricken look, as if she'd taken in a mouthful of guilt and couldn't swallow it.

Unlocking the door, he pushed it open and ushered her in. Totally by accident, his wrist grazed the swell of her breast as she moved past him. Her eyes instantly shot to his. Quicker than an electric short could cause a fire, high voltage shimmered between them. Gar couldn't help but notice that her mind immediately strayed off business—and fibs.

"So this is where you live? What are we doing here?"

"No one would admit to living in this disaster," Gar assured her dryly, "but if you'll cover your eyes, we're only going to be here for two minutes. I just need to pick up something from the bedroom, and then we're out of here."

He disappeared into the bedroom and left her stranded. So far, she hadn't raised any objections to being kidnapped for the evening. So far, he wasn't sure she'd noticed. But, Abby being Abby, he strongly suspected that the immediate loud silence emanating from the living room indicated she was too busy poking and looking around to worry about being railroaded.

He wasn't sure what she'd think of his place. The guest-lodge rooms had luxury appointments. Not his. The bedroom and kitchen parts of the suite were humdrum-ordinary, and the massive living room... Well. Bookshelves lined one wall from floor to ceiling, with books toppling helter-skelter, on subjects ranging from history to management to fast mysteries. His mother was an afghan maker, and her favorite habit overflowed on him. He had an oil painting from an artist friend on one wall—a nude—and some Japanese prints on another. They didn't go together. Nothing went together. The furniture beneath the debris wasn't too bad, but a screen sectioned off a plain old shop table with a wood lathe. Shelves held rough pieces of zebra wood, ebony, rosewood, cedar.

When he strode from the bedroom, carrying a black-cased hangar, he found Abby peering behind the screen. "You work with wood?" she asked him.

"Yeah, and I know it looks like hell in here, but as big as this monster lodge is, there wasn't a single place where I could set up a shop. Working with wood is my way of relaxing."

"I don't think it looks like hell—and it'd be nobody's business if it did. Everybody needs some private space. I've seen my fill of antiseptic upwardly mobile decorating—nothing you can touch, nothing you can do, no place to let down your hair and just...be." He could have listened to her leap to his defense for a couple more hours, but all too quickly she noticed the garment bag on his arm. "What are you carrying there?"

"A tux."

"Uh-huh. And the pope believes in reincarnation."

"Honest, it's a tux. And we're going from here to your place—you've got some glad rags and high-heeled sneakers in that closet of yours, don't you?"

"Glad rags," she echoed.

"Yup. We're going to need them for a boat ride."

"Glad rags. To go on a boat ride in the middle of winter." She touched his arm, as if offering comfort to the demented. "You're off your rocker, Cameron. All this time I thought you were a nice, sane, rational man—"

"You don't believe me?" Gar camped up an injured tone, which started her laughing. She was positive he wasn't serious. Almost. There were nerves in that laughter, which suited him fine. Keeping Abby just a little off balance struck him as the best idea in town.

Fair was fair. She'd unbalanced him from the minute they met.

He swept her back out the door, thinking that it was time he solved the mystery of who she was, what she'd done, where she'd been, that she hid so deeply. She protested about her nonbusiness background louder and longer than Shakespeare's Kate.

It wasn't Janet's type of lying, Gar had told himself a dozen times. Abby wasn't manipulative. She had nothing to gain, that he could perceive, from those incredibly inventive fibs she made up. But something in her life obviously troubled her enough to hide it.

There were ways to make that daffodil blonde come clean. Putting his arms around her was one. And throwing her off-kilter was another. Tonight he planned to do both.

Trust took time, Gar knew well. But his heart was

going on the line damn fast, and sinking even more damn deeply. And the relationship had no prayer of going anywhere unless she was willing to be honest with him.

Abby had assumed he was teasing about the boat ride. Even when he took over her upstairs bathroom to change into a tux, she'd just thought he had a more formal dinner in mind. And possibly her feminist philosophies had taken a short vacation to Timbuktu, because she loved his teasing her, loved his playing the kidnapping pirate and feeling swept off her feet.

As ruthlessly as he'd kidnapped her, though, Abby was coming to know him—and she should have suspected she had an unshakably ethical pirate on her hands. Gar had told her the truth about the boat ride.

As the paddleboat left the dock, the blue-green waters of Lake Tahoe churned into a froth. The blustery skies had cleared, opening a view of snowy mountain peaks and forested slopes against a fast-dropping red sun. Paddleboats ran on Lake Tahoe year-round, Gar had told her, and he'd thought she'd love one of the sunset dinner-dance cruises.

She more than loved it. The inside cabin gleamed with oak and brass, and a trio was already warming up on the stamp-size dance floor by the bar. Outside, it was colder than a well digger's ankle, but the view was so breathtaking she didn't want to go inside until they absolutely had to.

"I've never seen a blue like this lake," she told Gar.

"You'd better be careful, or you might just fall in love with Tahoe and never be able to leave. She has a long history of capturing even the toughest hearts. Even now...if you want to start a fight in town, just bring up all the ecological problems with preserving the lake. The funny thing is, from the old-timers to the money-grubbing new developers—we're all really playing the same tune. No one wants anything to happen that could harm the lake. We're all willing to fight to protect it.... Are you cold?"

She was freezing, but the look of him tempted her to shiver far more than any external temperature. Gar was leaning over the railing, as she was. The look of him in jeans could give a woman's hormones a rush. In a tux, he was a kissing cousin to downright dangerous. His shoulders stretched that tux jacket in a distinctly mean, lean, elegant way, and the contrast of those clear blue eyes and that shock of dark hair against his ruddy skin made it damn hard to look away from him.

"If I'm a little chilly, it's because you made me dress wrong, Cameron." She motioned to the passengers in the inside cabin. Some of the women wore dinner dresses, but plenty of the cruisers were clearly fresh from the ski slopes. No one was attired formally except for them. When she realized he was serious about the tux, she'd gussied up, teamed a white satin blouse with a black satin skirt, twisted her hair up and conned her feet into volunteering to wear killer heels.

"You like dressing up. I figured that out before, and I didn't care what anyone else was wearing. You're the only one I was having dinner with."

The wind was churling her hair, ruining the swept-up style. He chuckled as he reached out to steal the last of her hairpins. Her hair tumbled and whirled around his fingers. The look in his eyes was possessive, his touch as intimate and sleepy-tender as a caress.

Nerves churned in her stomach. When she was with him, she had this unforgivably helpless feeling that nothing else mattered but this moment, this man, and how they were together. Yet the past twenty-four hours had itched on her conscience like a mosquito bite. She hadn't forgotten acting like a panicked goose the night before. She hadn't forgotten Gar walking in on her and Robb, how he'd caught her exuberantly immersed in that business discussion. Everything she did seemed okay with him.

But it wasn't okay with her.

"Gar?" When he cocked his head in question, she took a breath. "I owe you an apology for last night."

"What for?"

"You know darn well what for." She straightened the lapel on his tux. "I'm sorry. For freaking out on you."

His dark eyebrows arched. "You didn't freak out on me. Your sister called. Interrupted the mood. And I don't think of either of us anticipated things were going to zoom out of control quite that fast. You had a right to say no. No apology is required, Abby. You weren't going to make either of us happy if you did something you didn't want to."

"I *did* want to. I just felt...anxious. That we were rushing, had never even talked about things. I wasn't prepared—"

Again he tucked a wild, wayward strand of hair behind her ear. "I was. I had protection...but I can't swear it was on my mind. And normally I'm a believer in getting those sticky, awkward questions out of the way long before they're a problem. You have a right to know I haven't been sexually involved with anyone recently."

"I haven't, either. That's why I didn't have—or wasn't on—any type of birth control."

"Abby?"

"What?" There'd been a smile in his eyes. A shared discomfort at having to handle those sticky, awkward questions. A shared understanding that neither of them was the kind to duck a problem just because it was uncomfortable. But that smile in his eyes died suddenly, and his tone turned grave.

"We've got to get you inside and out of the cold before you freeze to death. But I need to cover one more page in this book," he said quietly. "Maybe it wouldn't have crossed your mind, but it could have. I know I told you my ex-wife was involved with cocaine. She wasn't using needles, but in this day and age—hell, knowing she was on drugs and messing with a drug crowd was enough. I had myself tested, and retested. I have a clean bill of health. In fact, if you have any doubts or worries, I could show you the lab results—"

"Don't insult me, Cameron."

"Insult you?"

"My mom didn't raise any dumb daughters—and I'd have to be incredibly dumb to be involved with someone I didn't trust. I don't need to see any lab tests. You told me, that's the end of the matter. You'd never have gotten to first base—and we sure as patooties wouldn't be having this confounded embarrassing discussion—if I had any doubts about your integrity.''

Gar scratched his chin. ''What makes you so sure about that integrity? What makes you think I'm not your basic, average wolf on the prowl, hot for your bod and gone in the morning?''

She sighed, the sound lead-weighted with feminine dry humor. ''I *know* you're hot for my bod, Cameron. And I know about the integrity because I'm an expert on men.''

''Oh, yeah?'' A slash of a grin. ''You've been holding out on me. You didn't mention this whole long history with men before.''

She hadn't told him a lot of things—including that her whole long history with men had been limited to the business arena. Temporarily she sidestepped the devil's teasing by claiming starvation, and they went inside.

Night fell fast. They'd barely finished a glass of Pinot Noir before the cabin windows showed off a black-pepper sky studded with stars. Inside, brass gleamed and reflected off soft lantern lights, as waiters hustled to serve still-sizzling filet mignon. A trio with a bass, drum and keyboard started playing a mix of old and new nostalgic love songs. It was impossibly easy to let the whole romantic mood seep and sweep into her mood, but somehow that drumbeat of music thrummed in her mind like a warning.

Integrity *did* shine from Gar. She'd sensed it from the moment she met him. She'd worked with too many scoundrels driven by greed and ambition not to recognize a diamond. And it troubled her that she hadn't been equally up-front and honest with him.

The cabin buzzed with music and quiet conversation. When the waiter served coffee, she thought of the black-and-white cameo that Paige had made her. Her youngest sister claimed that a cameo had always been a symbol for truth.

Yet Abby wasn't sure she could define the truth anymore. She'd never failed at anything before being fired. Recognizing her mistakes wasn't that hard—and she was doing her 200% best to change so she'd never repeat those mistakes again.

But to admit to Gar about her failures, about being fired...she just couldn't seem to get the words said. Her shame seemed greater next to his own obvious personal successes. She couldn't imagine him loving a failure. And more troubling was recognizing how much his respect had already come to mean to her.

Lust alone wouldn't have been such a mess, Abby thought desperately. Maybe she wanted him. Maybe her hormones sang out-of-control arias if she came anywhere near him—but that was just the dangerous, wondrous power of desire. Much more terrifying was that she'd come to respect him. To admire him. And it was those nasty respect-and-caring elements that made her hopelessly aware she was falling in love with him.

"Hey," Gar murmured. "Is the cheesecake that bad?"

"Pardon?"

"You took one bite of that cheesecake and suddenly I saw this big broody frown—"

"No, no, it's wonderful.... I'm just really full," she admitted with a smile.

"Me too." He cocked his head toward the dance

floor. "It looks like twenty people are already packed in a one-by-one-foot square, but we could squeeze in there with them—"

Abby shook her head. "Trust me. You'd be risking your life."

"Is that a dare?"

She chuckled. "No, honestly—the truth is, I just never learned to dance."

That was when she realized that owning up to any such problem to Gar was a bad, bad mistake. He immediately stood up and hooked her hand. Threats of damage from her three-inch heels couldn't dissuade him. Neither did warnings of embarrassing both of them.

"You love trying new things," he reminded her.

That was true. Her competitive streak had always excited her into trying anything new—and usually barreling into it with 200% enthusiasm—but she just didn't want to risk bumbling and being clutzy around Gar. It didn't happen. The trio was playing a silky, sappy love song, and she discovered in two minutes flat that Gar didn't know how to dance any more than she did.

Neither of them had to know how. He noosed her arms around his neck and wrapped his around her waist, and they simply moved, cheek to cheek, pelvis to pelvis. The trio changed to a rumba. They didn't. The musicians tried some old rock and roll. They didn't. The miniature dance floor was so squish-packed that couples bumped them right and left.

She didn't see them.

She didn't hear them.

Every time she lifted her head, his eyes were waiting for her. His big hands were both supple and subtle, moving down her spine until his fingers rested on the swell of her hips…lower than they should be in public, low enough to press, just enough, so she could feel the heat and hardness of his arousal growing between them. Her breasts were crushed the same way against his chest, molding to him, as if her whole body were a puzzle piece that fit his in perfect belonging. Even behind that starched white linen shirt, he had to know how warm she was becoming, how shamelessly responsively her body reacted to the closeness of his.

Vaguely she became aware that the cruise was nearly over. They were coming back to dock. Others hustled to get a last drink, to find their coats. Not Gar. Not them. His cheek snuggled against her brow as if they were glued together. And though it wasn't wise, her eyes closed as she shuffled with him to music only they could hear, maybe music only they could dance to.

Abby couldn't even try to deny the magic. This was what she'd always been missing. Him. She'd always been hurt by the stereotype of ambitious women being tough and unfeminine, and she'd slowly, painfully, come to understand that she always secretly believed in that stereotype herself. So far, it seemed through her whole life, she'd failed and floundered at every traditional woman's role she ever tried….

But not with him. Some crazy, mystical thing happened every time she was with Gar. She felt exactly like the woman she'd always wanted to be. Pure female. Desired. Vulnerable, but exhilarated and high on those powerful feelings, too…just to be with him. Just to be touched by him.

Gar murmured, "If you rub against me any harder, Ms. Stanford, I may just give you more trouble than you'd appreciate in a public place."

"You're blaming me? You've been giving me trouble ever since we stepped out on this dance floor."

"You could have slapped my hand and told me to behave."

"Maybe I didn't want you to behave."

"I think you like taking big risks."

She lifted her head, the smile on her lips fading at the intense, dark look in his eyes. "Yeah, I do. I love taking risks, always have. But not this kind, Gar." She sucked in an uneasy breath. "This kind of risk is so rare for me that I can't even..."

"You can't even what?"

He'd stopped shuffling. So had she. Hell's bells, the trio had deserted the dance floor five minutes ago. The paddleboat was docking, noise and action all around them. Everyone was getting off. Still, he didn't move, and neither did she.

"I need to tell you something," she said quietly.

"So tell me."

"You've been so open about your life, your ex-wife, so many things. I know I haven't been frank the same way." She swallowed hard. "Gar, I did something that I don't want you to know. Something I'm ashamed of. I haven't meant to lie to you or hide something in some...devious sense. This is just a problem that I need to face and fix on my own."

"Talking about a problem can help, Abby."

She shook her head. "Not this. And I didn't bring up the subject to raise your curiosity...but because I wanted to be honest with you. I can't make you any promises right now."

His knuckles brushed her cheek. "Did you hear me asking for any?"

"No, but...I don't know where you think the two of us are going. And I don't want to mislead you. I'm not playing, Gar. Playing with your emotions, using you. I just really feel unsure about anything in the future right now."

"Abby?"

"What?"

"The future is a giant unknown abyss. And some decisions have a way of taking care of themselves. Where we're going from here, tonight, though, is damn clear to me."

Abby understood what he was asking her. He neither wanted nor intended to sleep alone tonight.

Neither did she.

She took his hand. And led him off the dance floor.

Chapter Nine

Her car was still at the lodge, but Gar wasn't about to drive her back there—to pick up her car or check on his business or for any other reason. He wasn't about to separate from her. He wasn't about to risk getting waylaid or interrupted, either.

His lady was in the mood.

He threw his pager in the back seat when they reached her place. She fumbled in her purse for the door key. Once inside the condo, he never had a chance to switch on a light—or strip off his tux jacket—before her arms flew around him.

That kiss was still coming on as she kicked off her heels, lowering her height a good three inches. He peeled off his jacket and heeled off his shoes, neither easy tasks to accomplish with his spine hunched over like a bow and his mouth still latched on hers—but severing the kiss wasn't an option.

He wasn't sure what had inspired this frenzy of a rush from her. Gar had no doubt a gentleman would take the time to ask her. It mattered. He cared. Just then, though, he figured they could talk about it intensively—tomorrow morning.

She claimed his mouth the way a guy dreamed a woman would kiss him. Wildly. Seductively. Her need for him was exposed and naked. Her mouth was open, wet, hot, her tongue ravishing his like a greedy, hungry thief. But possibly a thief on her first heist, Gar considered, because as breathtakingly as she'd taken charge of the excitement and danger parts, she was a teensy bit vulnerable in the planning department. Unless one of them moved things along, they might well end up making love against her front door in the dark.

Formulating a more coherent plan was challenging, when his brain was functioning at tumble speed. He lifted her, hooking her legs around his waist while their tongues were still dueling, her eyes still closed. He took three steps toward the stairs, then stopped. Making love to her in that sybaritic bachelor lair went against the grain. The damn bedroom not only had the distinctive stamp of another man, but made Gar think of cheap fast sex.

Fast sex was definitely on his mind. Very, very fast sex. Before he died from burning up. But cheap wasn't the nature of anything he wanted for Abby. He favored something extremely expensive. For her. For him. Something that cost so much that she wouldn't scare off or be able to walk away easily.

The living room might not be ideal, but it had the unbeatable advantage of being four steps away. Negotiating his way in the dark turned into a trickier adventure than he planned. The coffee table took a bite out of his shin, and a chair leg tried to trip him. She still had crafts and debris on every available surface…but not, thankfully, on the moonlit patch of thick plush carpet by the fireplace. He eased her down, his heart slamming so fast he could hardly breathe. The hearth still had a memory smell of woodsmoke.

His heart still had a memory of her eyes, on the dance floor, when she'd told him she'd done something she was ashamed of. He'd wanted her to be honest with him. But now that he had a piece of the truth, the interesting side problem emerged of what the hell to do with it.

Loving her struck him as the only choice that made sense. Loving her well. Loving her irrevocably and immediately. Eventually he needed to ferret out the rest of the story from her, but Gar had scraped his way too far in life to overworry the nature of the problem. People made mistakes. Even daffodil blondes with unshakable New England consciences who couldn't lie worth beans made mistakes. His ex-wife's recent and determined intrusion in his own life guaranteed that Gar was not into judging anyone else. No grown-ups their age escaped the scars of experience.

To Gar, that was what made love different. Being old enough to know what was worth fighting for. Worth *feeling* for.

And emotions were bleeding and kicking and pulsing inside him like he couldn't even remember, couldn't even try to define, but they all had her name on them. Kisses blended one into another, a spiraling sweep of restless, lush sensations with her taste, her scent, her texture. He'd known longing before. But not belonging. Not this hot, clawing need to belong to her, with her, those claws hooking him so deep that nothing smaller than an avalanche had better try getting between them.

"Gar..." Her eyes opened suddenly. Her voice was hoarse and thready.

"I'll take care of it." He assumed she'd opened her eyes because she caught a whiff of sanity and remembered protection. The rogue thought zoomed through his mind that he didn't want it. He wanted her bareback, nothing between them. And the thought of her having his baby—which sure as hell had been known to sabotage a man's mood—only fired his hotter.

"I wasn't thinking about protection," she whispered.

The comment did not precisely inspire him to put a lid on the rogue thoughts in his head. "I can't say I like the gift wrap. But it's ribbed. Nothing at all would be better, but—"

"Gar..." A smile, as swift and alluringly wicked as a tufty spring wind. "I wouldn't know a ribbed from a nonribbed. That's not my problem. I can't get your blasted cuff links off."

He could. But the cuff links took a battle, and so did the tux shirt buttons. Suspenders tangled and dangled when he finally tore the things off altogether. Either of them could have had the sense to turn on a light. Neither did. She fumbled with earrings and bracelet, and once the jewelry was gone, she reached behind her to unlatch the satin button at the nape.

He was freer by then. And when her arms were raised, trapped behind her neck, his mouth lowered to her breast. Through the satin blouse fabric, he felt the nipple pucker and tighten. His hand swept up her silk stocking, up her smooth thigh, up to her hip under the short skirt. When he cupped her fanny, she rolled on top of him, the project of removing their clothes temporarily abandoned.

Another jet stream of kisses wouldn't wait. Touching each other wouldn't wait. Hunger was leeching sanity from both of them. She moaned against his mouth. He groaned against hers.

Need this rich should be outlawed. Emotion poured from her, as if she'd been bottling it up for a lifetime, as if she didn't know what to do and every touch were a treasure to be savored and explored. He had the wondrous feeling, the ominous feeling, that making love with Abby was going to be nothing like any lovemaking he'd ever known. There was danger down that road, but he only wanted more of it, not less. More of her. Never less.

A telephone pealed from somewhere in the darkness. He heard it, but he had both palms inside her panty hose, her skirt twisted around her waist, her mouth sealed against his tighter than a promise. No, he told himself. It couldn't happen. Not a phone interruption a second time. Fate couldn't be that mean. He had to be imagining it.

The telephone pealed again.

Her head shot up. Her hair shimmered like a silky gold curtain; her eyes looked dazed and dark. ''I'm *not* getting it,'' she said fiercely.

But by then he'd sucked in a lungful of air, and a bite of reality with it. ''It's after midnight.'' When that didn't seem to register, he added, ''It's later than your sister called last night, really late for anyone to be calling—unless it were family or someone who really needed to get ahold of you."

Still she stared at him for a blank second. Then the phone rang a third time. He saw her swallow. Blindly he reached up, groping on the closest table for a lamp. Like a bad déjà vu repeat of last night, he nearly knocked over the ceramic monster lamp in the process of trying to locate the switch.

When he flicked it on, the sudden light glared harshly on her pale face. She was moving by then. She looked aggravated and frustrated enough to murder someone—preferably not him—but she nearly destroyed all hope of his potential future progeny with a knee, when she twisted around, trying to get up.

The receiver was on the other side of the room, buried under a needlepoint canvas and a pile of skeined yarn. Abby pushed the debris aside and grabbed the phone. It wasn't a moment when she felt capable of a polite hello. She barked, "This had better be Mom or Dad," with a dire threat of restitution in her voice if the caller didn't come up with the correct response pronto.

"No. This is Gwen. Oh, God. Oh, God. I couldn't possibly have interrupted something two nights in a row. You don't have to say anything, Abby, I'm going to hang up right this second and go shoot myself—"

Abby rolled her eyes. "You don't have to go that far. However—"

"I know, I know, I can tell, you have a guy there. I'm so sorry I could die."

"I never said I had a guy here, and you don't have to be sorry, you goose. But unless someone is dying or there's trouble in the family, I'll talk to you tomorrow...."

"Okay, okay." Clunk.

That clunk was a terrible sound. Positively Abby didn't appreciate the interruption, but as the connection was severed, she desperately wanted it back. Talking with her sister was at least nice and safe. The silence behind her was darn near deafening.

She didn't want to turn around and face Gar. Nerves *kathunked* and re*kathunked* in her stomach. The desire wasn't gone. Her pulse was still reeling, her heart still pounding, but moments before, her response to him had seemed romantic and natural and infinitely right.

Now she wanted to squeeze her eyes closed and disappear. Her satin blouse was gaping open, her bra undone and dangling, her skirt yanked up around her hips. She had to look like some sleazy, brazen...hussy. A vulnerably exposed hussy. In these past weeks, she hadn't once missed her dress-for-success power suits, but 90% naked was a heck of way to have to face a man who was undoubtedly both mad and frustrated. At the phone. At life. At her.

Knowing she had to, she swallowed a lumpful of courage—and spun around.

Yikes. She could avoid directly meeting his eyes for another coward's second, but the rest of the view was unavoidable. Gar was in worse shape than she was. He was still wearing pants. And one sock. But some nameless, shameless she-cat seemed to have hurled his expensive formal linen shirt into the hearth. His riveting expanse of muscular bare chest had a less-than-respectable bite mark near the shoulder. His tux suspenders seemed to be gracing a lampshade. She'd destroyed his hair. She'd...

She'd just about decided to go hide under the bed for a decade or two, when by accident, by mistake, her gaze connected with his. Once their eyes met, something made her heartbeat slow way, way down.

Gar's face, his eyes, had always mirrored the man he was. Laugh lines reflected his irrepressible humor; character lines mapped the weight and depth of his experiences, all the depth of emotion that had stamped his life. But not now. At that moment, his expression was stoic, his eyes were blank, and his shoulders were rigidly tense—as if he were coiled up and prepared to spring, get up and out, no different from the way he'd taken off the night before, when she asked him to.

Seconds before, she'd felt bumbling and unsure of what he was thinking, what he was feeling, how to possibly make this awkwardness come out right. But she sensed his aloneness, even if he'd never spoken of loneliness. And she saw a man who never expressed or pushed his own needs, even though he'd been incredibly sensitive to hers.

"Cameron..." She'd always trusted logic and rule books, never really believed in feminine instincts. Yet it was a woman's instinct that made her cock her head and try for a light, humorous tone. "I swear we're doomed. We've had the strangest bad luck with odd things going wrong when we're together. Flat tires, messes, interruptions...and I'll bet, especially this time, you think you're off the hook."

He still looked braced to leap to his feet, but the comment clearly surprised him. "Off the hook?"

"Uh-huh. The mood's broken. Yet again. And

maybe you're thinking, 'Aha, I get to go home now, this lady's more trouble than a bad penny and maybe it's a good thing I was saved by Ma Bell.'" Watching his eyes, she pushed away from the table and started toward him. "Well, I hate to break the news to you—but you're not saved."

"No?"

"No. You aren't getting out of this seduction just because of a little obstacle here and there," she said sternly.

"Aw, hell. Don't tell me I'm being threatened with a fate worse than death?"

"Uh-huh. And I'm afraid there's more bad news—"

"I'm not sure I can take much more."

There now, she thought. The stoic look was gone, the devil back in his eyes. And maybe it was the devil that gave her the courage to go for broke with some serious honesty. "Afraid you're stuck hearing this, too, Gar. I think we're both crazy. That's why I bolted on you last night. I'm afraid of doing this, afraid we're diving into a relationship where we haven't set any boundaries. I like boundaries. I like to read all the fine print on the rules. I'm damned scared that you could get hurt. That I could get hurt..."

Not only did his expression immediately turn serious, she saw his mouth open. So typical of Gar and his hopelessly protective nature—he was always going to respond if a woman expressed fear. She hustled to continue before he could get a word in. "But I want to make love with you. I've never thrown myself at a man in my entire life, so darned if I know how you got so unlucky. But that's your problem. You'd better brace yourself. Because unless I hear an immediate, bell-clear *no* out of you, here I come."

She didn't hear a *no,* but she saw those long, strong arms open wide. She was painfully conscious that he might bc counting on the wanton she-cat he'd had on his hands earlier. Therc was no way to explain that her wildness had come not from a woman confident in her sexuality, but from just plain old fear. Fear that those incredible feelings would dissolve in smoke if she dared stop. Fear that she was dreaming the wonder and power of emotion she felt in her arms. Fear that if she stopped for two seconds to breathe, she'd start worrying about her performance, if she was disappointing him, if she was woman enough to please him, and that old familiar enemy of anxiety would take over.

But nothing had been normal since the day she met him—and nothing was normal now. The same old monster woman-doubts were sitting right there in her head. But somehow...she couldn't seem to concentrate on them.

All those other kisses had been fast and furious; they were already too unclothed, and they'd passed too many bases, to go back. She knew those things for sure...yet Gar didn't seem to. He wrapped her in his arms with cradling slowness, and when he nuzzled in for a kiss, his mouth took hers with aching softness, as if her lips were tender and fragile, as if she were brand-new to him and he'd never known the taste or touch of her before.

Like a petal drinking in the morning sun, she opened for him. A slow, lazy kiss gradually turned deeper, darker, spun into something that spelled out yearning and longing. She knew his loneliness. Gar was strong, a man who valued control and took charge far more easily than he depended on anyone else. She had the same kind of strength, knew exactly that kind of aloneness, and knew that sometimes the loneliness could build up into a powder keg of stored-up, dammed-up need that ached inside you like...softness.

She couldn't remember any softness like the texture of his mouth under hers. No other softness compared to the sweep of his hand, tender, cherishing, as he peeled off clothes, slowly now, taking the time to savor...each response as she gave it. Each response as she learned it. Nothing had ever felt so new to her; she'd never felt free to reveal this terrifying and wondrous vulnerability with anyone else.

Since he seemed intent on torturing her, Abby considered that a gentleman should respect the rule about taking turns.

The tux pants, much as they elegantly accentuated his long, lean legs, had to go. She found an appendix scar on his abdomen, discovered a ticklish spot near his ribs, explored the shell of his ear with her tongue, rubbed her cheek against his furry chest. It was so funny. She'd always worried so much about doing things wrong, but those inhibitions seemed to have deserted her like fair-weather friends. Exploring him, learning him, seemed to have no right or wrong connected to it. It was a joy in itself. An end in itself.

Sort of. He groaned like a man in pain when her fingers closed around him. She looked up, interested in precisely what made him sound so miserable. His eyes were waiting for her. So was his mouth. He took a nip out of her collarbone, which might or might not have been intended to distract her from the fascinating loot her pirate hand was intent on claiming. It didn't. "You like this," she murmured.

"No."

"Oh, yeah, you do." She didn't need a stethoscope to pick up the heartbeat in that warm, hard flesh. A violently healthy heartbeat surged under her fingertips, and damn near went manic under the cupped caress of her palm. Odd, how touching him made her belly tight. Intimately, urgently tight. "Do we, um, remember where we might find that fancy ribbed gift wrapping?"

"It's around," he muttered.

A less-than-complete answer, she noticed. One might have gotten the impression that Gar was debilitated, at her mercy. It was a dangerous, perilous impression to give a woman who'd never experienced that kind of feminine power before. "Cameron, you're making me feel good," she warned him.

"Well, that's one of us. You're making me want to die."

She shook her head despairingly. "You obviously don't understand. You've got to quit encouraging me, or you're just going to end up with more trouble. Some women will take a mile if you give 'em an inch, you know...." She scrounged around, seeking the packet, guessing it had to be in either his tux pants or his jacket. When she came up with it, his hand reached out. "I'll do it," she told him.

"I don't think I can trust you."

"Take it to the bank. You can't," she promised him. "And not being overly familiar with this little chore, it may take me a couple hours to figure it out—"

"No, it won't."

"Is, um, one of us in a sudden hurry?"

"Yeah, you are, brown eyes." He twisted her beneath him faster than a magician's sleight of hand, and the rogue had that kind of magic in his eyes. Desire, like a hot blue flame. Tenderness, that coiled up the nerves inside her until they were close to bursting. How he knew she'd reached the limit of frustration was beyond her, but he was right.

She'd had enough play. And she could have sworn she didn't trust any man, even Gar, to really surrender control. Just in case she was terrible at this sex performance business, faking it seemed a far better idea than risking anyone knowing. She'd kept the secret extremely well from any other man.

Not from him. He wrapped her legs high and tight around him, then drove inside her with hot, thrilling force. As if he were tuned to her body's channel, he watched her, touched her, catching signals from her that she didn't even know she was giving. He started a taut, urgent rhythm that made her blood rush with exhilaration. Colors flashed in her mind, the glittery silver of fear, the rich red of sheer sensation, the deep, haunting blue of his eyes. His hands cupped the soft curves of her bottom, clenching, squeezing. She had no prayer of keeping the reins of control. Need simmered, shimmered, then boiled over into a realm where the hottest burn felt like the sweetest fire.

She'd felt need before, and for sure the loneliness of sexual desire and frustration. But not physical longing like this that stripped away all the civilized trappings. Shadows and lamplight blurred in her vision. She saw his skin take on the sheen of gold, saw the grave tension in his face, the impossible look of love in his eyes.

She *felt* love. For that moment, that was all she knew, all she was. She closed her eyes and swept into a free-fall, hurtling into a place where nothing existed but this primal, basic, vital need to belong. To him. To be taken, by him. To love—him. Only him.

"Don't wake up, Abby. It's so early it's still dark out. I just wanted to tell you that I'm leaving for work, and I'll take care of getting your car back to you later this morning—"

Only some things registered within the silken web of sleep. A column of dove-gray light. The scent of her toothpaste and shampoo on him, the rustle of his clothes, his hand, cool on her cheek. A vague understanding that, of course, he needed to go back to the lodge, but memories of the night cuddled her harder in a fantasy land between sleep and wakefulness. "Kiss first," she murmured.

It was only a sleepy demand, but it wouldn't end there quite so easily. Nothing in her life compared to his lovemaking the night before. Even half-awake, she felt as satisfied as a cat with the keys to the creamery, confident as a smug queen of Sheba. Since he was solely responsible for making her feel that way, Gar was the one responsible for the consequences. A kiss turned into trouble. Alluring, tempting trouble.

When he finally got up to get dressed a second time, he tucked the covers close to her chin, swore at her until she giggled, and then he kissed her one last time, with a bossy order to sleep in late.

She couldn't remember obeying an order since she

was three—and never willingly even then. But before she heard the door latch close, her eyelids dropped again. She snuggled into the warmth of covers that smelled like him, like them. Sometime in the night, they'd moved to the king-size bed upstairs. He'd christened the bed—and her—before falling asleep again.

Snoozing away a morning went against her puritan grain, but he'd wasted her. Deliciously. For the first time since she could remember, she felt...secure. Safe, secure, and loved—although the taste of that last word felt uneasy. Nothing was settled between them. No future was even on the table. Yet this was enough, she told herself.

There was no way the night before had been wrong or hurtful. For him. For her. No matter what happened, nothing could take away the wonder or the joy of her time with him.

Yet in the dark realm of sleep, a nightmare stirred. The same recurring dream had been hounding her rest for weeks now. She'd feel secure and confident that morning, too, striding into Jacob Dushanka's mauve-and-gray office, expecting to hear that she'd been promoted to his job.

Jacob had never been a friend, never strayed from the role of boss, but his long, gaunt face and shrewd gray eyes were as familiar to her as a roommate's. Ill health was the only thing that could force Jacob into an early retirement; he loved everything about the advertising wars. He had taught her everything she knew, thrown gauntlets in front of her to see what she was made of for seven long years.

Jacob was the toughest judge in town, but she'd proved herself to him; she *knew* she had. And that morning, when he briskly informed him that an outsider—a stranger, a man—had inherited the CEO job instead of her, she'd felt…a stab inside. Like the blade of a knife that pierced with the stunning betrayal of pain.

"So you're saying I'm fired." The word even burned like the sting of the knife.

In the dream, Jacob made an impatient gesture. "That's not the word that will go down on your job record. You'll have nothing but kudos to put on your resumé."

"Whatever words get used it amounts to the same thing, I'm out of a job. Fired." She gulped in a lungful of air. "All right, exactly what did I do wrong?"

"Nothing."

"I know I was more qualified than anyone else in the office. Exactly what qualifications or experience did this man have that I didn't?"

"My vote was in your corner, Abby. That's all I can tell you. The board wanted an outsider, fresh blood."

In the nightmare, she shook her head wildly, just as she had that morning. "I did something wrong. I must have, or I would have gotten the job. I'm not trying to argue with you, Jacob, but if I personally failed to do something, I need to know, need to understand…."

It wasn't anyone else's nightmare. Just hers. So many years of her life invested, snapped away in a puff of wind. Business was the only thing she knew. From the time she was a kid, this had been the one arena where she shone, where she experienced fistfuls of success, where she never doubted herself. And in the dream, she was suddenly standing mortifyingly naked in front of her sixty-year-old-mentor.

Jacob had never been kind, yet he tried to soothe her disappointment. Something was wrong with his voice, though, and the words came out like bullets.

He told her that this was just the luck of a bad draw. It happened. He told her that she was the toughest broad he knew. He told her that she'd proved herself as a cutthroat competitor. He told her all kinds of compliments, as Jacob defined compliments, and they were once words that Abby craved to hear.

But in the dream, they jangled. Jangled and jangled and jangled. She was naked, couldn't he see it? The cutthroat tough broad label lashed around her heart like the hurtful slice of a whip. She'd always been faking it. That was why she failed. Real women weren't ambitious, weren't doomed by this kind of drive and determination. She'd failed to be a man. Only she'd never wanted to be a man, just to be herself, her own way, and the sound of failure jangled in her heart like an incessant, merciless…

Abby's eyes suddenly popped open. Winter sunlight poured through the balcony door panes. The incessant sound hadn't come from her nightmare at all.

The phone was ringing.

Chapter Ten

The phone showed no inclination to quit ringing. Shards of the nightmare were still slicing through her mind as Abby fumbled for the receiver.

"So," her sister Paige said, with no preamble, "who is he?"

"Good grief. You've been talking to Gwen, haven't you?"

"He isn't still there, is he?"

Abby rolled onto her back, suddenly aware of how hard her heart was pounding. She just couldn't shake the stomach-dropping feeling that the nightmare had come back to haunt her for a reason. Last night had upped the ante on every risk she had ever taken with a man. When she was with Gar, everything seemed right—so right that she blithely and easily forgot about firings and failures.

But the nightmare hadn't scared her half as much this time as waking up to reality. Failing a stupid job seemed like a pipsqueak nothing compared to the risk of failing a man she'd fallen hopelessly, dangerously, in love with.

"You're aren't talking," her youngest sister scolded. "Is this guy still there?"

"No."

"But you're not awake yet." Assuming her yes, Paige started pelting out directives. "There has to be a traveling phone somewhere in the place. Go get it. You can brush your teeth and go nuke some coffee while we're talking."

"I hate to tell you this, but you're the squirt in the family. The low man in the hierarchy. The youngest, the one *we* get to bully and give orders to. I'm in the lofty oldest-sister seat."

"Uh-huh. I want a name on this dude. And unless you answer all the questions correctly on his being a good guy, I'm likely to fly out there to take him out."

Abby scrambled downstairs to claim the traveling phone, and hooked the receiver in her ear as she hit the kitchen, poured instant coffee and put it in the microwave. "How did I get two sisters with a secret Rambo streak?"

"Don't you give me any grief. All the times we've called you, not once—not once—have you ever had a guy sleeping over. We don't know whether to be happy for you. Or kill him. Either way, there isn't a prayer of us not prying. Now, I don't have to ask if he has a brain. You were never bowled over by a set of biceps. So he's smart and he sure as gold must have something going for him to level you—"

By then, Abby had hiked up the stairs and had a toothbrush in hand in the bathroom. "Excuse me? What is this 'level me' talk? Whose side are you on?"

"Yours, you dimwit. Now. Are we conceivably seeing orange blossoms and rings in the future?"

The toothpaste tube shot a glob of rainbow gel onto the mirror. "For Pete's sake, Paige. Nothing has remotely gone that far. Neither of us are thinking in that direction. We're just getting to know each other—"

"I'd say it's gone beyond that, if he spent the night. How was it?"

"Paige!"

"Spit out the toothpaste. I can hardly understand you. And I'm just asking in general terms. Like Gwen puts it, on a scale of one to ten, ten being Mel Gibson and one being you could have more fun folding the laundry."

She spit. Then scrubbed her face with a cold washcloth. But nothing seemed to wake her up well enough to handle this phone call. "Didn't we quit rating guys in junior high?"

"When we're talking to other grown-up women, yes. But you're talking to a sister now. Gimme a number, or I'll never let you get to that coffee."

"All right, all right. Five hundred and one."

"Holy cow." All teasing disappeared from her sister's voice. "Are you scared?"

"Yes."

"Bad scared, huh?"

Abby gulped. "Yes." It was a relief to say it. And although her sisters bullied and pried and interfered and teased, there was no one on earth she could have admitted that to but Paige or Gwen.

And Paige had the sensitivity—and love—to understand that she wasn't willing to talk further about the subject, because she dropped it. By the time Abby was downstairs, and pulling the mug of coffee from the microwave, her sister had moved on to another topic. "You've been in Tahoe for a month now. Have you made up your mind what you're going to do next? Are you looking for a job, and what's happening with your place in Los Angeles?"

"My lease isn't up on the L.A. place for another couple months, but I know I'm not going back there to live. I need to make a trip and box things up, get the place closed up."

"So when do you plan to do that packing-up thing?"

Abby gulped down several sips, wishing she could inhale the caffeine. "I was thinking about going back in a couple of weeks, definitely before the end of February. It's not like I have to rush, but it's hanging over my head. I'm trying not to push myself into forcing a job decision—or even job hunting—until I'm ready. But closing up the apartment has to be done. I know positively that I don't want anything to do with a big-city life-style again."

"You know you can come and camp here for as long as you want, don't you?"

"Yeah, sweetie, I know. And for the record—even when you're being a total pain in the keester—I love you, sis."

"That's mutual," Paige said gruffly, and then hesitated. "You still beating yourself up about that job?"

"Um...some."

"I figured you were. And I hope you don't rush

into another job, any other job, until you've really taken a serious break.'' Paige paused again. ''You know, I was thinking the other day...about how the three of us were so dead positive what we wanted when we were girls. We each started out on one road, and ended up doing something entirely different. But I don't think we were *wrong,* Abby. I just think women's roles are complicated in the nineties. And as we grew up and changed...the truth of what we wanted changed, too.''

Even after they hung up, the conversation lingered in Abby's mind. When she hiked upstairs to get dressed, her gaze lanced on the onyx-and-pearl cameo her sister had made for her—black and white, a symbol of truth, and Abby had always been a relentless truth lover...until she was fired.

When she lost the job, it had seemed she didn't know what the truth was anymore. Maybe she'd sold herself a lie about what really mattered to her, but finding a new direction for herself was not so easy. As hard as she was trying to change, to turn herself around, every woman's role she tried seemed to fit her no better than a hand-me-down dress. She'd screwed up by giving a career too much importance, but her humorous debacles with cookie making and crafts were outright failures on the traditional homemaking front, too.

Pensively Abby strode across the room to touch the smooth carved profile in the cameo. The woman had an inner glow. Not beauty, exactly, but a look of serenity that reflected a joy and confidence from the inside out. It seemed exactly what Abby had always searched for. Serenity. A feeling of being at peace with herself. It never mattered whether she could make cookies—or get a CEO position. What mattered was becoming a woman she could respect and like.

Those answers might come in time, but her sister's phone call jolted her into realizing what she was doing with Gar. They'd made love. That irrevocably upped the ante from a casual relationship to a potential serious one. Abby had no regrets. Last night, Gar had more than touched her heart. He'd touched her soul. But it was one thing to fall in love with a preciously special man—and another to selfishly risk hurting him.

Abby hadn't forgotten that his ex-wife had been an unhealthy, dependent woman, floundering in life. The last thing he needed was another flounderer. He needed an equal. And Abby needed to have the integrity to either come up to snuff and get her life together—or get off the playing field and leave him free to find someone who could.

She turned away from the cameo and started burrowing into drawers for clothes, thinking, *Two weeks.* That wasn't a lot of time to force answers from herself, but the trip she needed to make to Los Angeles would make a natural break point—if there had to be one.

Gar had been forthright from the start; he wasn't looking for a casual affair. And neither was she, but Abby had never anticipated that a man could capture her heart so swiftly, so completely. If she couldn't control her feelings for him, she could at least control her actions. Her mind laid down indelible ground rules. She could be with him for these two weeks. She could do things for him, with him—as long as those things were clearly positive in his life. As long as she didn't disappoint him.

A woman had badly disappointed him before who was floundering in life. She couldn't let it happen to him. Not again. And of all the things she'd seemed to fail at lately, none were worth a plugged nickel compared to this. She had the painful, dread-anxious feeling that to fail Gar was to fail herself as a woman—at a level she'd never understood before. At a level she wasn't sure she could recover from.

Gar stood in the doorway and rubbed the back of his neck. When he returned from a late-afternoon meeting with his banker, half the staff had reported that Abby was around. The chef claimed she'd poured a mug of hot chocolate for herself in the restaurant kitchen. Robb claimed she was talking to Simpson in the downstairs lobby. Simpson claimed she was in the upstairs office talking with Robb.

Lots of people had seen her. But he'd followed all the leads as faithfully as a cop after a murder suspect, and come up with no body.

Until now.

Technically the office was the first place he should have looked, since this was where he'd set her up with a computer and desk space days ago. Heaven knew what had made Abby change her mind so fast—particularly as she was still claiming to have no forte in business—but she'd taken on "playing" with a public relations program for the lodge with bulldog determination and racehorse speed. He'd never wanted her to work that hard, but it was like trying to stop a moving train.

Still, he hadn't thought to look in the office, because of the hour. It was almost eight at night, blacker than a thief's heart outside, the wind howling up a blizzard storm. It was time for normal folks to have dinner dishes done and be curled up in front of a sitcom.

He didn't live normal hours. Neither did she. But he'd just never expected to find her holed up in front of a computer terminal this late. Her hair looked like a silvery-gold curtain in the eerie monitor light. A long black sweater made a dramatic contrast to her ivory coloring and blond hair. Desire stirred, just from looking at her—but that wasn't headline news.

"What," he said from the doorway, "do you think you're doing?"

"Skiing," she answered him. She flashed him a welcoming "hello" smile, but her eyes darted right back to the computer monitor.

"Funny, you don't look like you're skiing."

"That's how much you know." With her gaze still glued to the computer, she lifted one long, shapely leg—and pulled up her pants cuff. "Is that the mother of all bruises on my shin, or what? And I've got another award-winner on my fanny—although I don't believe it'd be politically correct to show you that one at the moment. I'm getting good on the slopes, Cameron."

"So I hear." He was almost hearing a report on every breath she took from his employees, all of whom she'd won over like a witch weaving a magic wand. He had a good staff. A fine staff. But no one had ever won over Robb and Simpson, and Jennifer had been known to screech bloody murder if any outsider set foot in the kitchens—except for her. "Did you, um, realize it was eight o'clock?"

"Can't be," she assured him blithely. "I came in

off the slopes around three, freezing, just thought I'd pop in here and play with some marketing ideas for a couple of minutes while I warmed up.... Your cousin is adorable, isn't he?"

The last Gar noticed; the subject on the table was her problem with losing track of time, not his family tree. But he played along. "Which cousin?"

"Ryder."

"Adorable? Are you kidding? Ryder's fat, prematurely balding, and short as a fence post."

"Now don't try selling manure to a horse trader, big guy." Her fingers clattered on the keyboard nonstop. "I may have only talked to him on e-mail, but I know men."

"So you keep telling me." It was another of her infamous fibs, as far as Gar could tell. She hadn't been a virgin that first night they made love, but her lack of experience had come as a stunning surprise.

So had her responsiveness—that night, and the four nights since. Abby was slowly, dangerously and maybe irrevocably insinuating herself into his mind, his nerves, his heart. She made love the way she did everything else. Total immersion. 200%. Forget the obstacles and ignore any risk. Unfortunately, she tended to tease him 200%, too.

"So what gives you the idea that my baby cousin is adorable?" So she wouldn't miss it, he stressed the "baby."

"I just know, that's all. And for the record, he asked me to marry him."

"Beg your pardon?"

"Just on e-mail, and don't be raising your eyebrows at me. If you hadn't told him to introduce himself to me via cyberspace, it'd never have happened. He's a real e-mail flirt." She sighed humorously, but then turned serious. "Cameron, he's a lamb in the woods. A brainchild. So cute. So bright. But so naive. And I need your help. We were just chatting about his new business, and I offered him a couple ideas—nothing, really—and I got a note from him that he's sending me a thousand bucks and putting me on retainer."

"So what part in that scenario do you need my help for? The marriage proposal, or knowing how to cash a check?"

"Handling the marriage proposal was nothing. I told him I weighed three hundred pounds and was built like a Hummer."

Gar scratched his chin. "That could present a real interesting problem if you meet him in person."

"One crosses one's bridges when one comes to them," she said judiciously. "And what I want your help with is the money. I don't want his money, Gar, and he's just getting this company started. I just offered him a little friendly advice, that's all. I don't know one thing about the gadget thingamabob he's manufacturing. Which I told him."

"Uh-huh." She'd told him a lot of things, many of which would take a magnifying glass to find a grain of truth. The more he was around her, the more her background and natural bent in some field of marketing was obvious—and so was her love for that kind of work. Yet she persisted, vociferously, in claiming a total dislike for anything to do with business.

Honesty mattered to him, way too much, for him to ignore this tiny problem he had with her. Yet he was slowly coming to understand that Abby wasn't precisely fibbing to him—or to the rest of the world, but more to herself. For reasons he couldn't fathom, she seemed determined that broccoli would turn into carrots if she just said it aloud often enough.

Gar suspected the base of the problem had to be that mysterious "thing" she admitted to being ashamed of. So far, she'd ducked the subject faster than quicksilver whenever he tried to bring it up. Initially he'd guessed that the problem had to be a man—maybe a married man, something hairy like that—because Abby definitely had one of those staunch New England consciences, and the problem had to be seriously dicey to wrestle that kind of shame from her.

Initially, he'd also figured that he was gonna hate the story, and really hate the guy. But judging her had never crossed his mind. Gar, too, had made mistakes of his own. If he could just coax her into bringing the problem out in the open, he couldn't imagine anything she'd done that they couldn't get past...or handle together.

Time had passed since Gar first reasoned that out, though, and he'd since concluded positively that his first guesses had been wrong. The problem wasn't a man. Couldn't be. She seemed too stunned at her own responsiveness in bed. She was a poignant contradiction between terrible shyness, and honest wildness. How such a naturally sensual, earthy lover of a woman could be so unfamiliar with the pleasures of her own body was beyond him.

He decided he might get enough of her. By the twenty-third century.

In the meantime, she obviously intended to get off

the computer, because she was standing up with her fanny in the air—but her fingers were still clicking those keys.

"Stanford," he said sternly, "I'm going to unplug the computer if you don't turn it off."

"I am, I am—"

"You have to be hungry. Think food. Think a nice glass of wine, and dinner, and a decadent chocolate dessert—"

"Chocolate!" That did it. She punched the save button and exited, grabbed her jacket and purse, and was at his side faster than a racehorse at the Derby.

"Nothing works with you half as well as bribery," he teased. Hooking an arm around her shoulder, he steered her out the door and toward the lobby. "We can eat wherever you want, but I want to head upstairs for a couple of minutes, if it's okay. I've been in this suit all day, just want to change in something more comfortable."

"No problem. And how'd the meeting with your banker go?"

"Long and boring. All it takes to make a banker happy is giving him money. It's no fun when there's no challenge...." As they passed the front desk en route to the elevator, Gar cocked his head toward Simpson. "What did you do to my receptionist?"

"Simpson? Nothing."

"I hardly recognized her when she showed up for work this morning."

"Oh, that. She looks wonderful without the extra five pounds of mascara, doesn't she?"

"You told her to tone down the hair and makeup?"

Abby's eyebrows arched. "Heavens, no. I'd never

tell another woman what to do. I think everyone's entitled to their own sense of style. But we were sort of casually chitchatting about how heavy makeup can appear...defensive. Like you're hiding behind it. And there are certain guys who'll pounce on you if they sense you have a weakness...."

"And?"

"And she has a lot of guys pouncing on her. The wrong kind of guys. She came to her own conclusions about throwing out the circus paint, Gar, I really had nothing to do with it...."

So Abby claimed about everything else she'd done over the past few days. That first morning, Gar hadn't been sure what made her change her mind about coming in. But she'd popped in "for an hour" and never quite gotten around to leaving. The next day, she'd come to ski—and had—but had somehow ended up paired with Robb, poking her nose in every cranny and cupboard in the lodge. And today was no different from the others. She'd come "to play." And ended up working slave hours on this public relations program for him.

Twice, she had bluntly and carefully asked if she was intruding. She'd gotten all nervous, hugging her arms, said he needed to be frank with her—she didn't want to be in his way. But she only had about two weeks of straight vacation time left, so if she had any serious chance of coming up with some good marketing ideas for him, she really needed to know more about the lodge and how it was run.

Gar didn't object to her knowing a damn thing, and she wasn't remotely in his way. Hell, there wasn't an employee in the place she hadn't charmed. He was the only one who never seemed to see her.

But her mentioning that "two weeks" had come back to haunt him. Usually, when a couple made love, the woman half of the pair hustled to pin the man down. Abby seemed to be warning him that their relationship had an end point—that was coming up ominously and imminently fast.

Right now, though, she wasn't running. As soon as he unlocked the door to his suite, she dropped her things on the couch and aimed for his minifridge. "You want a beer? Or a glass of wine?"

"I want a kiss."

"Honestly. Men." She bounced to her feet and swung her arms around him with a cheeky grin—and a big scold. "Don't try taking more than one, Cameron, until you feed me."

But she gave him more than one. The first was a sassy bird peck, but he hadn't kissed her all day, for God's sake. And she never came close enough to even brush his hand, not in front of his employees or anywhere near people in the lodge. He respected her sense of decorum...but he liked stripping it away from her even more.

She'd missed him. Maybe it was his imagination that she was scared of this relationship and planned to fly. She never kissed him like she was going anywhere, ever. Her mouth molded under his, softer than whipped cream, tasting him, teasing him, taking his mouth, no different from the yearning, hungry way he took hers.

She pulled back her head. Eventually. And muttered, "Dammit, Cameron," which about summed up his immediate problem with frustration, too.

"Are we, um still hungry for dinner?"

"No," she said dryly. "But it's not like that problem's going anywhere, and I know you've been on your feet since daybreak. You need food. And a chance to wind down, I think."

"I *would* like to take a quick shower and get out of this damn suit—"

"So go. I'll pour myself a glass of wine and catch some CNN. I'm perfectly fine on my own. Take your time."

He had no intention or interest in taking his time. Peeling off the suit and a hot, fast shower couldn't have taken him ten minutes. He attacked his chin with an electric razor and pulled on jeans and an old black sweater, mulling over how she took care of him. It wasn't like she overfussed. She just had a way of assessing his mood and picking up whether he was tired or revved up or whatever.

She was 500% woman, right to the bone, Gar mused. But her feminine perception, her instinctive way of showing caring, was subtle, not intrusive, not demanding. He hoped he was the same way with her from the masculine side of the fence, and he couldn't stop thinking of how good they were together—good for each other—and how already he couldn't imagine her *not* in his life long-term. *Slow down,* he mentally warned himself.

But when he strode back into the living room, he expected to find Abby slowed down...and instead, she was pacing in front of CNN, holding her jacket in one hand, and his in the other. The instant she spotted him, she announced, "We're leaving."

"What's wrong?"

"You didn't hear the phone ring?"

"I thought I did once, but between the shower and the buzz of the electric razor—"

"Uh-huh. Well, there've been three calls. All women. Your ex-wife. Then a woman with a dark, sultry voice by the name of Narda. Then a peppy little redhead-sounding voice by the name of Suzanne." She tossed him his jacket. "I put your answering machine on. Your other women are simply going to have to get ahold of you another time. You, Buster, are coming with me."

Chapter Eleven

Once they left Gar's lodge, starvation was the first problem that needed solving. Abby admitted to taking charge, but somehow a simple dinner plan had accidentally become a little...decadent.

Heaven knew, she was striving to obliterate the workaholic side of her character and become a lazy, laid-back hedonist. Until now, this worthwhile goal had been a total failure. She was *trying*. But mastering laziness refused to come easily. She didn't do "idle" well. Shaking loose the wholesome, responsible—boring—side of her personality had been backbreakingly hard work.

Tonight, though, she was tasting her first heady flavor of success. Her gaze wandered around the bathroom. Two vanilla candles flickered from the shelf of the square malachite tub. A few feet away, a fat peach candle reflected a teardrop flame in the long vanity mirror. Whirlpool jets thrummed a rolling surge of hot water. The piped-in stereo played Tchaikovsky's *Violin Concerto in D* barely loud enough to hear, but still music to bring out the winsome romantic in the most hopeless cynic. Steam whispered around the semidark room, clinging to the rich emerald-green malachite, dancing around the candlelight, carrying the scents of peach and vanilla into the shadows.

The white cartons of Chinese lining the tub shelf seemed a tad out of place. Eating dinner in the bathtub, in fact, had initially chafed against all of Abby's New England puritan nerves. It was disgraceful. It was sinful. It was silly.

But it was working, Abby mused dryly. She'd only been joking when she brought up the idea to Gar. The thing was, when they finally caught up with each other around eight, she'd caught the strain lines around his eyes, the tense muscles in his shoulders. He was more revved up than an overheated engine. She'd lived a workaholic's hours too many years not to recognize the symptoms—he'd had a good workday, just too long. Maybe he was whipped, but it wasn't that easy to turn off the power switch.

Gar had outright laughed when she suggested the whimsical idea of eating Chinese in the bathtub. He hadn't taken the outlandish idea any more seriously than she meant it, but he'd started relaxing with that laughter...which was exactly what he needed to do. And it wasn't half as hard as she expected to jettison her New England puritan nerves and follow through, when the rewards for misbehaving were right in front of her eyes.

He was naked now. He'd staked out one corner of the tub, she had another, and beneath the concealing bubbly water, their toes touched. Both of them had knees raised—knees were hardly substitutes for tables, but they successfully balanced cartons of Chinese and chopsticks pretty well. Glasses of white wine glowed in the candelight. His skin looked as burnished as a pirate's. Water droplets riveled over the smooth hard slope of his shoulders, droplets that sneaked into his wiry chest hair and hid there.

Her gaze had a nasty tendency to stray toward his body. *Not* a good idea, when looking at him inspired a hopeless hormonal reaction, and just then she didn't want to be distracted. She was no pro at chopsticks. Gar was, and most of that hard-edged tension had slowly seeped out of his muscles. But not all. They still had one teensy thing to discuss, she suspected, before he would—or could—completely relax.

He'd leveled a pint of shrimp fried rice and another of steak kow before he got around to bringing it up.

"Um, about those other women calling me..."

It was the first time Abby had ever seen him nervous. She decided even a saint couldn't have resisted stringing him along just a little bit. She raised her eyebrows. "You're naked with me in a bathtub and you want to discuss other women, Cameron?"

"Actually, it seemed the most logical time—considering I was already in hot water up to my neck." Gar cleared his throat, then blustered on. "You were right about Suzanne being a redhead. She's my broker. And she tends to call me at night because I'm hard to reach at a desk during the day. She's about fifty, fifty-five, married thirty years, two grandkids—"

"Uh-huh. Pass the war sui gui, would you?"

He checked the row of white cartons perched on the rim of the malachite tub and handed her the appropriate one, but his eyes homed in on her face with a watchful wariness. "Narda...she's a little more awkward to explain."

When Abby dived into the war sui gui without further comment, he forged ahead with that awkward explaining. "I've known her almost from the time I moved here. In the beginning, we went out just to see if it was going anywhere. In more recent times, we'd occasionally call each other if either of us needed a convenient date, some function or occasion where it was easier to walk in as a pair. She's nice—great sense of humor, a lot of fun. A friend. You'd like her. In fact, I think you'd like her a lot."

"Uh-huh." Abby lifted her glass over the swirling, steaming water. It wasn't like Gar was in a mood to accommodate her, but he moved faster than a spring-loaded trigger to grab the wine bottle and pour her a refill.

"She never did call often. And since we were never more than friends—casual friends," he rapidly qualified, "she had no reason to know you were in my life."

"Uh-huh. So your married broker likes to flirt with you on the phone, and this Narda is seriously gorgeous and occasionally lets you know she's hot for your bod—"

"Did I say either of those things?" Gar asked the ceiling. "I'm almost positive I never said either of those things."

Poor baby. Possibly she was savoring his being miserable—just a little bit—but enough was enough. "Listen, you, I never thought you were hanging out in a monastery until the day you met me. You're a successful, single, eligible, adorable bachelor. Unless the women in Tahoe are all myopic, my guess is you have women giving you a rush quite frequently."

"You think I'm adorable, huh?"

She rolled her eyes. "I'm *trying* to explain why those women calling you didn't give me a royal cow. I can get into jealousy. I just tend to see it as a low-return investment. Worth indulging in, but not worth getting in a major sweat over. A lover who'd cheat on me would be out the door—nothing to be jealous about, because I wouldn't want any more to do with him. But that's a different situation. I can hardly hold you responsible because the ladies in Tahoe have good taste in men."

"I completely agree," Gar said gravely, which earned him a splash and a tickling assault with her toes.

He started laughing. Abby did, too, but she wasn't quite ready to end the conversation. She was well aware that he'd started out the evening with another source of stress. Maybe the subject was quicksand, an area where a new lover had no right to intrude. But Abby had yet to see Gar vent a problem on anyone else, including her.

She understood self-reliance and control and pride. She had all of them in abundance. Which, fortunately or unfortunately, made her uniquely aware of how stupid it was to take those things too far.

"Gar...you can tell me to put my foot in it, if you want," she said hesitantly. "But your ex-wife was one of those callers. I take it she still doesn't seem inclined to leave you alone?"

He sobered quickly. "No." He rubbed a tired hand at the back of his neck. "It's mighty tempting to tell you that I've found a brilliant way to handle the problem. But so far, any brilliant answers seem to elude me."

"I think I quit believing in brilliant answers when I was around twelve. Nothing in adult life is ever that easy," she said gently. Even in that soft, shadowy darkness, she could see something in his eyes that made her pause. "Well, damn...have I somehow made this worse? Has she increased these calls because of me in some way?"

"I don't want you worried about it, Abby. It's not your problem."

"That didn't remotely answer my question, big guy."

He sighed, not without humor. "Because of the night she walked in on us, she's aware you're in my life," he admitted. "Hell. She has no legal—or moral—right to know anything I do. But it seems to be bugging her. For some reason, it never seemed to occur to her that I would be with someone else."

It burned like a bee sting, that she could have accidentally added to the problems with his ex-wife. Abby hadn't forgotten the promise she'd made to herself. Either she was good for Gar or she had no business being with him...and he'd already had an overdose of floundering women who couldn't stand on their own. "So she's more than giving you hell. She's being a serious plague?" Abby murmured.

"I've tried listening to her. I've tried cutting her

off. Doesn't matter what I do. It's like getting through to rock," Gar said dryly. "If push comes down to shove, I can try the obvious legal recourse and check out what constitutes a harassment charge—"

"But it would really bother you to do that." Abby had no trouble intuiting the why. "It'd go against your sense of honor, wouldn't it, Cameron? You've got quite a dragon on your back about protecting women. No matter what the provocation, I can't see you choosing to be tough with a lady unless you absolutely had to. And you're probably worried she isn't real stable on the drug front, that she could tip one way or another—especially if she's showing you less-than-stable behavior with these calls."

She felt his eyes on her face, almost softer than a caress. "You don't have to be this understanding, Abby. But you got the whole nutshell. I have no interest in encouraging her, but I just don't want to feel responsible for anything she might do."

"And you're not, Gar, but what you *are* doing is being way too tough on yourself. Just do the best you can, you know? If she really won't quit, maybe you'll have to make tougher choices. But as long as she isn't driving you outright nuts, you don't have to leap into some action that doesn't feel right to you. However..."

"However?"

Abby felt she was about the least qualified person on earth to give advice on his ex-wife. It was more than time to move to less dangerous subject waters. "However...I keep thinking about your suite at the lodge. Not that it isn't a stupendous place, but I can sure see that it's pretty impossible to escape from stress there. I mean, you have no place where you can shut off the phones. Relax and put your feet up for real. Wouldn't you like a yard? A place with a shop for your woodworking?"

"Look who's talking. You're camping out in Don Juan's lair."

She chuckled. "Well, that's the truth." She leaned her head back against the cool, smooth tiles, as he had. "It took about two seconds flat before I was happy being spoiled with the hot tub. But that den-of-iniquity bedroom with the cheesy fake furs sure isn't what I'd choose on my own."

"So. If you could build an ideal place, what would you pick?"

"Hmmm." She took a last sip of wine and let it swirl on her tongue. "I dunno...a porch with an old-fashioned swing. Soft colors, maybe not pastels, but no stark black and whites, for absolute positive. Thick carpets, because I like being barefoot in the house..."

"An easy-care kitchen..."

"Definitely a must. And lots of closets, so it's easy to get stuff put away and out of sight."

"I want a workshop. Long. Well lit. Where I can lock the door and shoot anyone who tries to come in."

Abby chuckled. "Me, too. I don't want a workshop. But I always thought the ideal house would have a private place—an office or whatever. That was just *my* space."

"No purple," Gar said firmly.

She had to grin again. "You have a thing against purple?"

"I love my mother. But I swear, I grew up purpled to death. *No* purples."

"Well, if you're gonna get picky...I can't stand pea green."

"No purples. No pea greens. How many bedrooms you want?"

"Hmmm. That's tricky. Even a dream house shouldn't be such a monster size that it's tough to take care of, but I'd still want some spare bedrooms for company...times like holidays, my family tends to descend en masse."

"Mine does, too. But what about bedrooms for kids?"

"Kids?" she asked blankly.

"Children," Gar said succinctly. "Those little things that start out in diapers and never stop talking and make sticky messes? You want any of those?"

His voice was lazy and light, teasing. So had hers been, yet this strange lump suddenly lodged in her throat. Once upon a time, her answer to his question would have been easy.

She'd always wanted children. Her parents, her sisters, had always been everything to her. Growing up, she'd always pictured herself having the same kind of family, a house filled with noise and laughter and sibling squabbling and love. Definitely love.

Ambition and her drive for achievement and success had postponed those dreams, but initially Abby had assumed there'd be time for a family a little later. Over her years in business, though, that dream just started...eroding. The higher she climbed the corporate ladder, the more she was treated a certain way—by men and women, no different. If she was ambitious, she must have more testosterone than estrogen. Her femininity was suspect. She couldn't be *normal*. Aggressiveness was admired in a guy, but no one loved a woman with the same qualities. Respected, yes. But definitely not loved. And those invisible messages over the years had kept adding up—if she was good at business, than she must be flawed at doing the traditional woman things. Like being a mom. And a homemaker. And somebody's wife.

She felt Gar's eyes on her.

And forced herself to swallow that sudden thick lump in her throat. Pictures flashed in her mind, of her cooking and baking debacles, of the failed crafts scattered all over her living room—but she banished those from her mind, too.

There was no reason to think Gar intended something emotionally loaded by his question about children. They'd just been making idle chitchat about an imaginary ideal house, kids in general. The whole personal identity crisis she was going through was not Gar's problem—nor did she ever want it to be.

He was relaxed now, his arms stretched out on the rim of the malachite tub, and it was so rare to see him indulging in some serious laziness. The foolishness of eating Chinese in the bathtub had done the job. It was exactly what she'd wanted, what she'd hoped—to do something for him for a change. To be good for him. The way he'd been incredibly good for her. And absolutely nothing else was supposed to be on this night's agenda.

"Um..." Gar's voice suddenly dropped an octave. Possibly because he'd discovered her toes traveling in some unexpected places. "Why do I have the feeling that we're not still having a conversation about dream houses?"

"You can talk about houses," she assured him.

"Well...but somehow my mind is suddenly less on houses and more on the imminent fear of drowning."

"You can't swim?"

"I can swim."

"You're afraid of a little risk?"

His eyes gleamed. "I think one of us is asking for serious trouble, Stanford."

It positively couldn't be her. She'd always been a problem-solver, not a problem-causer. Which she told him—primly and firmly—right before she scooched across the hot tub to claim a kiss.

He was smiling when she kissed him the first time. But his skin was slippery. Hot. Distracting the man wasn't even a marginal challenge, yet, amazingly, a simple, mischievous kiss turned into another, then another. And suddenly she was the one distracted.

He dragged his mouth against hers, stealing her tongue. It was just play, still play, that stealing and dueling of tongues, but his hands discovered places to skate and slide that lacked any claim to child's play. She was close enough to rub her slick, warm breasts against his slick, warm chest, to taste the water droplets on his shoulder, his jaw. A candle dribbled down to its base and flickered out. Fragrant smoke and steam drifted together, and their corner of the room was suddenly darker and more intimate. She could hear his breathing roughen, hear the burbling, bubbling water, but nothing seemed louder than the pounding of her own heartbeat.

Nothing could happen. She was sure. No matter how huge the tub, it was still square, with no conceivable way to stretch out, no conceivable way to...

Midway through another dragging, drugging kiss, he pulled her on top of him. Water sluiced and sloshed as he maneuvered her on his lap, her knees tucked around his hips. Blood rushed through her pulse at a fresh gallop. It seemed Gar had a slightly different vote on what could or couldn't happen. Cradled on his lap, she could hardly fail to feel his interest in the project grow and harden. It was something like sitting on a hammer. A warm, pulsing hammer.

"You're going to kill me," he murmured once, his voice as rough and hoarse as if he were a man suffering from fever.

Maybe fever was her problem, too. Her old friend Anxiety hadn't shown up with Gar before, but her heart was firing frantic pistons of nerves now. She was a take-charge lady, but not in this. She didn't know what to do in this position, felt fumblingly awkward and afraid of failing him, and where his body was mostly concealed by the silky, silvery water, hers was painfully, vulnerable exposed. This was exactly the kind of nerves that always made her freeze up. Only...

Only that fever kept sweeping her under, sabotaging that whole intelligent, commonsense train of thought. It was all Gar's fault. Gar had put the goofy idea in her head that she had power—the feminine power to please him, to entice him, that he wanted her to do those things, that she could.

And damn the man, but she just couldn't keep her mind on worrying about failing him. The look in his eyes seemed to hot-wire all her sensible logic. Water lapped at their heartbeats as he lifted her, watching her response as he slowly, intimately filled that aching hollowness inside her. He felt silky. Hot. Huge. And she suddenly felt liquid from the inside out, her pulse gamboling, charging like a wild colt who'd just discovered freedom. She couldn't catch her breath. He wouldn't let her try.

In the satin darkness, his palms cupped her breasts, lifting them, kneading. He whispered, "I love you." He whispered, "You're beyond beautiful, love." And then he whispered something angry with frustration, and by then she was so rattled and so hot that she started a rhythm without thinking.

There was only him at that moment. Not the outside world. Not any of the things she was failing at, grappling with, struggling over. She wasn't failing him, because she was hopelessly, helplessly, part of him, instead of separate. What frustrated him, frustrated her. What pleasured her, pleasured him.

She knew how to love him. The stunning realization scissored through her pulse, slicing through inhibitions, cutting past fears. She trusted Gar, maybe more than she did herself. This wasn't need like a weakness, but need as bright and vital and strong as life. She felt strong with him. She felt love, wrapping her up in his secure arms, and something inside her bolted free on that wild rock and ride.

She'd have laughed from sheer joy, if desire wasn't clawing at both of them by then with sweet, wet, erotic teeth. Her muscles tensed for that first crash of pleasure that somehow spiraled into another and another. Colors exploded behind her eyes, no black and whites, but rainbows instead, jeweled colors flashing light and sensation.

And then she fell against Gar with an utterly exhausted splash.

* * *

"Listen, you lazy slugabed."

"Hmmm?" She heard Gar's voice, but she was still half-asleep and enjoying a dream replay of crashing on his chest in the tub the night before. The splash. His throaty laughter. And then his stroking her, stroking her, as they both struggled to breathe normally again...

The slap on her fanny made her blink awake.

Positively she preferred the dream over reality, Abby mused. Last night he'd treated her like the most precious treasure he'd ever found. He'd told her he loved her in a way that made a fist squeeze tight around her heart. A fist of longing. A fist of incredible wonder.

So much for love. When another swat on her backside failed to rouse her, the devil started pulling away the nice, warm, thick blanket. And then the sheet. "You dog," she said groggily.

"Now, now. I made you breakfast in bed. Doesn't that give a guy some brownie points?"

Unwillingly she opened her eyes, and had to instantly squint against the mercilessly bright sunlight. But she saw the tray and its contents. A fluffy omelet with fresh mushrooms. Toast, dusted with cinnamon and sugar. Coffee thicker than sludge. "Good grief, you're scaring me, Cameron. I wasn't born yesterday. You must want something."

"Sheesh, is the woman suspicious or what?"

"I trust you implicitly," she assured him. "But no man goes to this much trouble from the goodness of his heart. Whatcha want?"

"Nothing. But, um, I would appreciate it if you'd eat fast."

"Uh-huh. I knew there was something on the man's mind," she told the coffee, but her gaze was drawn to him like a thief tempted by an open bank vault. Some things a woman just couldn't be expected to resist. "You're not only dressed, but fresh-showered, fresh-shaved, shoes on, yet... What on earth time did you get up?"

"Six. I started thinking about everything we talked about last night. Houses. Moving. A place of my own. So I called a real estate agent—"

"At six in the morning?"

He fed her the toast to hurry her along. And then sabotaged his own efforts by kissing her between bites. "It was a friend, a guy I play racquetball with, already knew he was an early bird like me. Anyway, I have to be back at the lodge by noon for a meeting. But Russ told me about a house that's just going on the market that we could get a first look at this morning."

She swallowed quickly. "Did anyone ever mention that you move at the speed of light? Wouldn't you like to think about this for a long, lazy twenty-four hours before making a giant move like this?"

"I'm not making a move. But real estate can come and go damn fast in Tahoe, especially if it's a good place, and Russ seemed to think it was a prize. I just want a look-see, but I'd really like your opinion, rather than checking it out alone."

"So you've got a meeting at noon, and you want time to house-hunt, and it's—" she checked the bedside clock "—nine o'clock now. So I take it I've got three seconds flat to finish this incredible breakfast and get dressed?''

''Hey, I wasn't going to rush you. You can take at least five minutes,'' he said magnanimously.

Abby hurled a pillow at his head with a laugh—but she also engulfed her breakfast and threw on clothes faster than the speed of light. She had no idea if he was serious about the house hunting or if this was just a ''play'' outing. But she didn't care. She wanted to be with Gar, but not here, not anywhere near the malachite bathtub or the rumpled big bed—not for a little while.

They'd made love almost every night since that first unforgettable experience, but for her, the morning after was different this time. She didn't want to talk about it—not about his words of love, not about everything last night had meant to her. But she felt as fragile as a naked newborn this morning. Not unhappy. Just... vulnerable. She'd recognized before how deeply she'd fallen in love with Gar, but not how powerfully different her emotions were for him than they'd been for any other man...and how different *she* was, with him.

She badly needed time to think about that, seriously and alone, but being with him on this house hunting outing was even better. This was just about fun, about being friends together, where she felt much more sure of him—and her.

The day was vibrantly cold and brilliant, the sun so bright it put a spun-sugar glaze on the fresh snowfall. Gar picked up the key from the real estate agent, and they drove up the west side of Lake Tahoe. The landscape grew wilder, less civilized, with striking peeks of the turquoise lake nestled between hilly woods. A winding private drive led to the house, and Abby was charmed at the first view. The house was stone, two stories, with an open deck wrapping around the second floor.

When Gar unlocked the door, she stepped inside and started inhaling the place. Dust motes smoked in the sunlit windows. The house and property both were as quiet as peace. "It's undervalued," Gar told her. "Russ said a doc owns it, but he took a job in a hospital in another city, so the family had to move quickly. Nice, huh?"

"It sure is." She toured all of it, upstairs and down, poking in closets, hunching down to peer in cupboards, even freezing her nose to take a long, studying look at the unheated garage and man's workshop built over it.

They met up again in the front hall. "So what do you think?" Gar asked.

"I think it's a splendiferous place." She came close enough to flick a speck of lint from his navy blue sweater. "But not for you, big guy."

"Not for me? I like it. And there's all this stuff I thought you'd love—a room for a private office, kind of soft colors, no black and whites, a great porch...."

"There're lots of features I loved, but just too many things that wouldn't work well for you." She motioned toward the living room. "Great room. Terrific view. But there's no place to fit a long couch in there, and you're six-three—you need a long couch."

She led him back to the entryway. "No place to hang up your jacket or put a pair of wet boots, which means you're stuck tracking in dirt, and cleaning it up all the time."

"Bad idea, huh?"

"A total nuisance," she agreed.

"The shop's incredible."

"Yeah, I know I'm no judge of that, but it did look terrific. But there just have to be other places where you could either build or find a ready-made workshop, Gar, that didn't have so many disadvantages. There's miles of wasted hall space. And I'm guessing you have tons of skis and sports stuff—all that kind of paraphernalia you guys seem to accumulate. There's great storage upstairs, but almost none down. Nope," she said firmly, "it's just not convenient for you."

"Well, that's the last time I go house hunting by myself. I wouldn't have noticed any of that." Gar was chuckling as he locked the door behind them. When they climbed into his Cherokee, he peered through the windshield to take one last look at the place. "Abby?"

"Hmm?"

"What was your place like in Los Angeles?"

He slipped the question in so casually that she never hesitated before answering. "Wrong," she said dryly.

"Wrong in what way?"

"It's hard to explain. When I first rented the place, I thought it was perfect. And maybe it was, for what I wanted then. Right now, I'd just as soon never see it again...but, of course, I have to. I know I mentioned that I have to drive back there in a week or so. I left without making any arrangements or closing the place up."

"You decided to leave there suddenly?"

"Yeah, I did," she admitted.

Gar started the engine, but let it idle. Until that moment, for Abby, their whole morning had been an idyllic extension of the night before. She'd felt such a natural joy being with him that realities in the real world seemed back-seat-irrelevant—a dangerous illusion, Abby knew. And when Gar suddenly pushed on a pair of aviator dark shades, everything changed.

"So what happens after you sever your last ties in L.A.?" he asked bluntly.

Nerves clomped in her stomach with heavy feet. She'd have felt easier if she could have seen his eyes and had some clue how seriously he meant the question. "I don't know. Down the pike, I need a job, but I don't know where or what. Although it must sound irresponsible, I'm trying not to let myself make any decisions until this break is over. Gar..." She hesitated. "I'm not deliberately being evasive with you. I'm just doing the best I can to cope with a mistake I made. I don't want to go back to the life I was living in L.A. That's all I'm sure of. I'd give you clearer answers if I had them."

"Abby..." She heard the edge of frustration in his tone. "What do you think would happen if you tried trusting me? You think I'd turn tail and run if you confessed a problem?"

"No." The sharpness in his voice somehow made her own turn softer. "I think you're a hard-core white knight, Gar. You'd likely try to rescue me—or at least help."

"Then, dammit, what are you afraid of?"

She didn't have to dive deep for that answer. It was lying right on the tip of her heart. "I'm afraid of disappointing you."

"Maybe you couldn't."

"Cameron, I disappointed *me*. Big-time. And I'm having enough trouble living with that." Until that instant, she hadn't put it in black ink in her mind.

Weeks ago, being fired had seemed the epitome of a personal failure. Ironically, it seemed like a good thing now. If she'd never lost the job, maybe she'd never have taken a serious, hard look at the shallow, superficial directions her life had taken. Being blind, lying to herself, was the failure that really mattered.

Abby was grappling every which way to redefine who she was as a woman, to get her pride back, her self-respect. But through all the mistakes she'd made, she'd never hurt anyone but herself.

Only now she'd fallen in love with the best man she'd ever known, ever dreamed of knowing. Gar's respect mattered desperately to her. So did his love, even if she was afraid to admit it. She was trying her damnedest to face up to her own mistakes. But she simply couldn't face...failing Gar.

Chapter Twelve

If the U.S. president had shown up in the lodge restaurant, Gar doubted his chef, Jennifer, would poke her nose out of the kitchen. Her cooking skills were legend, but her whole personality defined the word *antisocial.* The last time he saw his chef within screeching distance of the public had been three days before—when Abby stopped by for lunch.

Typically for a Thursday evening, the restaurant was crowded when he spotted his chef blasting out of the kitchen, carrying a generously heaped tray—and snarling at a waitress who offered to carry it. Jennifer, much as he loved her, had shoulders of steel, the hips of a battleship, and a bosom that could justifiably be registered as an assault weapon.

It surprised him not at all that the tray was intended for their table. Gar leaned back just in time to avoid a direct bosom assault in his face as Jennifer started serving. It was a near-smothering miss.

When his chef finally straightened up, his eyes narrowed on the dishes in front of Abby. He'd gotten broiled chicken—which he'd asked for. Abby had gotten a baby filet—which she'd asked for. But next to Abby's plate was a slice of devil's food cake with marshmallow frosting—*and* a double fudge brownie slathered with hot caramel sauce.

"Hey," Gar protested. "How come she gets her dessert with dinner? And how come she gets two desserts? What about me?"

"You're just the boss," Jennifer informed him. As if this relationship made him as no-account as a gnat, she patted Abby's shoulder. "If he gives you any trouble, you just call me, dear. I raised four sons, I know how to put a man in his place. And if there's anything else you're hungry for, you just sing out, sweetheart."

"Thank you so much. Everything looks wonderful," Abby praised, making his chef beam and blush like a schoolgirl before blasting back to her kitchen.

"I don't know what you did to win her over, but I wish you'd sell me the patent. I haven't seen an ounce of respect from that woman since the day I hired her," Gar grumbled.

Abby's eyes danced with merriment. "Now, now, she worships the ground you walk on, Cameron. She told me herself, she thinks you're one hotsy-totsy dude."

"I'm not sure what 'hotsy-totsy' means, but talk is sure cheap. If my cook thinks I'm such a cool dude, how come *you* get the chocolate cake and I get all the sass?"

"Aha! The real truth comes out. It was never respect you wanted. It was the chocola..." Abby was having a ruthlessly good time teasing him when her voice abruptly trailed off. Her attention was suddenly riveted by a man standing in the restaurant doorway.

Near the end of the dinner-hour rush, another customer strolling in was hardly headline news. And normally, Gar might have felt a bite from the green-eyed jealousy bug at having a tall, dark, good-looking stranger capture her attention.

In this case, he used the excuse to steal a forkful of her chocolate cake...and to watch her.

She was wearing cocoa tonight. A simple enough cocoa tunic and slacks, but the color warmed her cheeks and made her hair look like spun honey. She'd added some personal style touches with a coral scarf and teardrop earrings. She never overdid makeup or clothes, never wore anything flashy, but Gar had yet to see her in public looking less than elegant and put-together. Poised. Prepared for anything.

Even when her mouth was gaping open.

"Gar...I can't believe this...." With her gaze still latched on the stranger in the doorway, her fingers groped blindly to pluck his sleeve.

"Hmmm," he murmured. No further response was required. She was busy, studying the man, frowning in concentration—which left Gar perfectly free to apply that same intense concentration on her.

She hadn't avoided him since the morning they went house hunting. The opposite was true. They'd spent every afternoon skiing, specifically on his competitors' ski slopes, because Abby claimed an inside understanding of the competition was critical to developing an effective public relations program for the lodge. Gar would have sworn in court that his lover had exuberant energy instead of blood in her veins. She'd wasted him on the ski slopes—and he was the one who knew how. Then come home to vent more of that incredible energy on him in an entirely different sport—again, one where he'd started out being the pro and her the novice. But she was gaining on him. Damn fast. And unforgettably well.

Abby yanked a little harder on his sleeve, but Gar was totally uninterested in the man scanning the room from the doorway.

She'd thrown him an unexpected curveball last night, he mused. She was innocent in the strangest ways. He'd have had to be blindly insensitive not to notice the teensy signs of crabbiness coming on, the tenderness in her breasts. But for some bewildering reason, the darn fool woman assumed he'd treat her like a contagious leper once she got her period.

She'd been pretty miserable. He'd dosed her with a glass of red wine and turned the light out early.

She'd slept in his arms, inseparable as glue, turning to him in the night as if she were afraid he'd be gone if she didn't hold him close...but she'd bolted out of bed in the morning.

As far as he could tell, she'd been bolting ever since the morning they went house hunting. At the time, he'd thought—hoped—that looking at houses might inspire the outlandishly wild idea in her mind of their living together. A future. Kids, rings, a backyard, the whole shebang. But no. She'd inspected that house with shrewd perception and incredible thoughtfulness, but it had all been directed toward whether the place would suit him—alone.

That was how Abby did things. Giving, not taking. He'd never met a more loving woman. Loving to him. Loving with him. She sensed his moods as if she had radar, gave endlessly, generously, not just in bed but in everything they did together.

And it had gone too far. Every time they turned a new corner onto closeness and intimacy, Abby brought up her upcoming trip to Los Angeles as if looking for any excuse to fly. It made no sense to Gar. She seemed happy; he knew of no reason why she'd be afraid of the incredible relationship developing between them…

Except for that secret in her past that she guarded closer than gold. Desperate men, Gar mused, could be driven to come up with desperate solutions. Unless he did something to make that damn secret come out, he was afraid she damn well would fly. And God knew if this would work, but he had to try *something.*

The man finally spotted them from the doorway and immediately strode in their direction.

Abby's fingers clutched his sleeve, yanking hard this time. "Gar, would you pay attention? This is the strangest thing. I know it sounds crazy, but there's a man coming toward us who looks exactly like you."

Not *exactly,* Gar thought critically. To a point the Cameron men tended to look alike—all of them were built lean and tall, with the same dusty brown hair, blue eyes and rocky jaw.

His cousin, though, was six years younger, and had inherited the lion's share of the good-looking genes. Ryder had a brash, cocky stride and a dimple in his cheek that had charmed every damn woman who ever laid eyes on it. Unlike himself, Ryder was not to be trusted around the ladies.

But his cousin could get a woman to talk more easily than any man on the planet that Gar had ever known.

"Hey, cousin." Ryder slapped him on the back. "You're not looking too bad for an old man." That greeting out of the way, he ignored his favorite first cousin completely and yanked out the chair next to Abby. Blue eyes sipped her in from top to bottom. A dazzling smile announced his verdict of the view.

He sank in the chair as if overcome. "You have to be Abby. You're the one I came to see, and my God, you look incredible for a woman who's lost two hundred pounds since I talked to you on e-mail last week."

Abby sputtered with laughter. "I should have realized you two were related the instant I saw you in the doorway. Gar put you up to this, didn't he?"

"No way," Ryder assured her. "No, no, don't waste time looking at my bounder of an aging cousin. You and I are the ones who have business together. You returned my check, darling," he said mournfully.

"Of course I did."

Ryder checked the table, reached over, and absconded with Gar's glass of wine and the rest of her chocolate cake. "I wasn't sure why you had a problem working with me, but communicating via e-mail has its limitations. I figured if I showed up in person, maybe I could convince you I wasn't such a bad Joe. I shower every day, use deodorant, don't bite—unless a lady asks nicely. More to the point, I'm respectful—"

"I can see that."

"Especially respectful when someone has a talent I don't. Which you clearly do..." Ryder took out the chocolate cake even faster than he talked. "Now this is my problem. I'm a smart man. My cousin'll vouch for my I.Q. But the fact is, I'm smart about math and engineering, and damn near a dimwit near anything to do with marketing. All those ideas you sent me on e-mail—I like them all."

Gar had watched his cousin in action before. Ryder had always been so full of hell that half the world didn't get it when he was dead serious.

Abby did. She was squirming in her seat the instant Ryder brought up that check, the same way she always reacted near the subject of business. She got all excited and animated and enthused. And then she got tense. No different this time; she never lost her poise, never lost her smile, but Gar watched her hands drop to her lap in a white-knuckled clasp. "Ryder, I was just talking with you, shooting the bull. Nothing I meant for you to take seriously."

"Call it whatever you want to. I want to use your ideas. And I don't see how that's right unless I pay you for them. Furthermore—because I'm so damned brilliant—I know it's not just ideas, but knowing how to implement 'em, that can make the difference in a successful business." Having vacuumed the cake, Ryder looked over the rest of the table for more loot. He absconded with a roll. "So. I want to pay you for the ideas, and the implementing part, too."

"Ryder, you don't just hire someone, or pay them, without having a clue what their qualifications are."

"Well, now, I interviewed a couple guys with

M.B.A.s. They talked more mumbo jumbo than politicians. Your ideas made horse sense, and we weren't doing any more than casual brainstorming. You're welcome to tell me whatever qualifications you either have or don't have. But cards on the table, I already heard all I need to know.'' The men never looked at each other. Ryder busied himself lavishly buttering the roll. ''I'm thinking a year. I just need a little help getting my baby on her feet. And this is the part, dammit, that I don't know how to do. You wouldn't have to be there, Abby. Between a phone, fax, and modem, you could be doing the work from anywhere. I'd pay you to make one trip, though, so you could see my setup.''

Abby shook her head with a throaty chuckle...but Gar saw her hand suddenly press on her stomach. ''I think you Cameron men have a little steamroller in your genes. Neither of you listen to me—''

''But that's exactly what I want to do, darlin'. Listen to you. I admit I'm in no position to offer you full-time work. At least yet. But I'd pay you well. You don't like money?''

''Everyone likes money. But—''

''You're already working so many hours that you can't spare a few more?''

''It's not that.''

''What's the problem, then?''

''The problem is that you're trying to bamboozle me,'' Abby said dryly. ''I don't make decisions this quickly. If you want me to think about the idea, I will—but I'm not going to give you answer this minute. And if you touch my caramel-covered brownie, you're not going to make it out of this restaurant alive."

Ryder carefully lifted his hand from her brownie plate and glanced at Gar. "Eek. She's got a mean streak, huh?"

"Tough as a pit bull," Gar affirmed.

"Beauty, brains, and tough, all in one package. Abby, are you *sure* you don't want to marry me?"

Her fast response made Ryder laugh, but Gar couldn't help but notice that the rest of dinner went the same way. She was never short of a quip, never short of a chuckle, and she handled his wayward rogue of a cousin with the skill of a lion tamer. Ryder had notorious lady-snowing skills. Abby wasn't snowed. She also wasn't eating. She pushed around and rearranged the food, but he never caught her taking a bite—even from her favorite brownie.

Around the time a second cup of coffee was served, she lifted her napkin to the table. "If you're flying back home tomorrow, Ryder, you two cousins probably want to catch up. I'd love to supervise—a pretty terrifying thought, what kind of trouble you two could stir up male-bonding all by yourselves—but I have to admit, I'm really beat. I need to head home..."

Ryder vociferously protested her leaving, making Abby chuckle, but she pushed back her chair. When Ryder stood up and offered a handshake, she gave him an affectionate kiss instead, and listened to his warning that they'd be talking soon.

Gar fetched her coat and his own, ignoring her argument that he didn't need to waste time walking her to the car. Her Lexus wasn't parked that far away, but the night was a mean subzero, and he made her zip and bundle up tight before pushing through the doors. Her face was pale by then. The sudden frigid blast of cold air flushed some color into her cheeks, but her skin still looked as translucent as porcelain, her eyes swimming and dark.

The restaurant had been people-bright and warm and noisy. They stepped outside to a different world. The night was still as glass. The stars looked like diamond chips, glittering against the inky-black sky. No sound intruded on that sudden quiet except for tires crunching on snow from an occasional passing car. When she shivered, he tucked her into the snuggling curve of his shoulder, and pressed a kiss on her temple as they walked.

"So...what'd you think of Ryder?"

"I think he's hell on wheels, could railroad anything in his path, has more charm than a lethal weapon, and I sure wouldn't want to be the woman stuck with the job of settling him down." She summed up, "I'm crazy about your cousin. I think he's a darling."

Gar chuckled. "Growing up, I admit I was inclined to kill him a couple of times, but I like him, too. Get past the nonsense, and he's a good man with a good heart."

They'd reached her shiny black Lexus. She dug in her purse for the key. "You set me up, Cameron," she announced quietly.

Gar heard no anger in her voice, yet he could feel himself bracing for a confrontation. Maybe until that moment he hadn't realized how frustration had been building up, like a stew pot suddenly boiling over. He was afraid of losing her. And he damn well didn't intend to lose her without a fight. "Yeah, I did," he admitted. "I didn't talk Ryder into coming here—no one talks my cousin into doing anything. But I knew he wanted to come, and I knew he was serious about offering you a job."

"You could have warned me ahead."

"Yeah, I could have. But I think you've paper-trained puppies before, whether they were wearing Armani suits or were still wet behind the ears. I'd have stepped in if I thought you were feeling pressured, but it was entirely up to you whether you wanted to say yes or no to my cousin's job offer—and I think you could handle a couple of Ryders with both hands tied behind your back. There was no reason for me to interfere."

"Handling him wasn't the question. Why you didn't tell me was the question."

"Because I needed some answers, Abby. About where you're coming from and where we're going, and damned if I can get you to talk to me." Gar heard the sudden harsh impatience in his voice, and shut up. Her head was dipped down while she was searching for the car key, her golden hair swirling around her cheeks like a curtain. But once she found the key, she lifted her head.

She looked at him, silent for that moment, hesitating.

There'd been excitement in her eyes when she was talking business with Ryder. Excitement, energy, a fired-up can't-sit-still anticipation. Until those liquid-brown eyes had abruptly turned deeply troubled, and she shut herself down like a revved-up engine suddenly cut dead.

Gar didn't get it. And though siccing Ryder on her

had never been an answer in itself, the encounter had affirmed what he already knew. However seriously Abby needed this vacation break, she wasn't happy being idle. She needed work. And no matter how goat-stubbornly she evaded any specifics about her business background, her knowledge and experience were as obvious as the sun rising in the morning.

When Gar was a kid, the way to get the alligator under the bed to disappear had been to turn on the light. He didn't know if she'd take Ryder's offer for work. Or his own. He didn't know why the whole subject of work was such a stress load for her. But Gar saw no way to flush out those damn alligators if he didn't at least try turning on a light.

"Gar." She lifted a hand, and with ice-cold fingers stroked the lapel of his jacket. A couple passed by them, laughing, holding hands, making noise. All he saw were her liquid eyes. All he heard was some damn message in her face that he couldn't read. "Have you ever failed at anything?"

This was the alligator? "Of course. A hundred things," he said impatiently.

"I mean, something serious. Something that really mattered to you."

"I failed at a marriage, Abby. You can't get much more serious than that."

"She failed you. You might feel responsible, Cameron, but she failed you. It's not the same thing." She dropped her hands, took a breath. There was a load of anxiety in her voice, a weariness, that he'd never heard before. "I never expected to go through life and always be able to avoid making mistakes. But respect is important to me. Self-respect. Your respect. I need to feel I can hold my head up. No relationship can work where both people aren't coming into it...equal. Can you understand that?"

"No." He grabbed her arms when it appeared she was turning away from him, toward the damn car. Adrenaline was charging through his veins. He didn't like that dread and sadness in her voice. "I don't understand, because you've made damn sure I couldn't. *Equal* is a stupid word. Nothing is equal in life. So you made a mistake. You think I'd be your judge and jury if you told me what it was?"

"No."

"I'm thirty-six. You think I don't know what mistakes are?"

"I know you do."

But there might as well have been a veil coming down over her eyes. It wasn't the first time she'd shut him out. But something in her face was different this time. And it made his voice harsh and rough. "I love you. And I think you feel the same. But I want more than a lover, Abby. I want a mate, a wife. A life together. I can't make you trust me, but there's a limit how far I can go with this. I need you to be honest with me."

"You're angry—"

He immediately loosened his hold on her arms, and forced himself to simmer down. "I made the mistake before—of allowing a problem to hide and fester. It won't work. It never works. I want a reason. Why you won't talk to me."

"It's not you, Gar. It's just that I have a problem I have to solve on my own."

"That's horseradish. Everyone needs help sometimes."

"Gar, you'd rescue the whole world if you could, and certainly you'd rescue a lady in distress. I'm not afraid you're going to judge me. I'm afraid you'll try to help me."

"That doesn't make a lick of sense."

"It might, if you could try and stop being so mad—"

"I'm not mad."

"Yeah, you are. You're furious," she said gently. "And I don't blame you. You never asked for anything but openness from me, and I know I haven't been. But nothing seemed that simple. I heard everything you told me about your ex-wife, and why honesty was especially important to you. But the story about your ex also made me realize that you don't need another woman unhealthily dependent on you. Needy. If I can't come to you whole, equal, then I'm getting out of your life." She squeezed her eyes closed and then turned swiftly, pivoting so fast she almost stumbled.

"Wait—"

The face she lifted to his was ghost-white. Pride-white. "I'm freezing and I want to go home."

She *was* freezing. Shivering hard. And a blasted public parking lot was no place to talk—or fight. But this fight, as far as Gar was concerned, was nowhere near over. His heart picked up a thready, uneasy beat, with a premonition that he shouldn't let her go; it was too important that they work this out, now, and no waiting for later. Yet he wasn't sure. She'd revealed mountains more than she had before, and maybe it would help him garner ammunition if he had time to assimilate and think about what she'd said. "I don't want you going anywhere if you're upset—"

"You've got Ryder waiting for you—"

"My cousin can fend for himself. I don't want you shook up because we've been arguing. It's just a fight, Abby, just something we need to work out, nothing more. It doesn't mean I don't care or—"

"Oh, Gar. I love you." She'd never said it before, and the words shut him up instantly. So did the swift, smooth, tender kiss she blessed his mouth with. The kiss was softer than spring. Alluring, like her. Sweet. Like desperation. That damn kiss scared him witless.

And then she climbed into the car, made her Lexus purr to life and was gone.

He'd call her first thing in the morning, he decided—and then zapped that thought in a second flat. The morning was too late. He'd never manage to wait that long. It couldn't take her fifteen minutes to drive home, and he'd call as soon as she could possibly get in the door.

Everything would be all right...Gar could surely find a way to make things right...if he could just talk to her again.

Chapter Thirteen

Abby initially intended to drive home. No different from a dozen other times, she turned left out of the lodge parking lot and aimed for her condo. When her Lexus zoomed past the turnoff road and kept going, she still had no real intention of leaving town.

It just seemed that her Lexus was rattled and riled up and all upset. She tried allowing the car to vent some of that high-strung energy on highway 80 out of Tahoe. Didn't help. Hours later, it was still chewing up the road, even after a cop had stopped her for a speeding ticket, even after she hit the turnoff from 80 around Sacramento. Neither the pitch-black night nor the long, lonely miles of blacktop seemed to appease or soothe the darn car. She had to stop for gas and aspirin for an incessantly pounding headache. Or maybe it was a pounding heart she was suffering from.

Her Lexus didn't seem to notice the difference. By the time the car merged on the Pasadena Freeway coming into Los Angeles, the sky was lightening from nightmare-black to pearl gray. She'd pitched her down jacket in the back seat long before then. The air was brisk, but certainly tons warmer than the February blizzards in the mountains. The smoggy fog and laddered superhighways made California seem like a separate planet from the high, dry, white-clean mountains and air in Tahoe.

Abby kept waiting for the sights and sounds and smells of L.A. to hit her as comforting. Every view was familiar. She'd spent seven years inhaling the city and calling it her own.

And when she unlocked the door to her old apartment and stepped in, she told herself this was really a brilliant choice. Maybe the breakneck drive had been impulsive, but she'd planned to make this trip within a matter of days anyway. She'd left mail, bills, the whole business of her life, hanging when she took off for Tahoe, and something had to be done with her furnishings and belongings before her lease ran out. There was no crisis about it, but the job had to be done. And right now, a nice, mind-boggling and exhausting physical project struck her as the best idea in town.

More to the point, her Lexus had kindly put a solid eight hours and five-hundred-plus miles between herself and Gar. She certainly wasn't running away, either from that anxiety-powered argument, or from him. As Abby saw it, she was removing a serious and unsolvable problem from his sight.

Namely, herself.

She pushed off her boots and threw down her jacket and purse. There seemed to be an ominous lump in her throat the size of Georgia. All those long driving hours hadn't cured the problem, but she'd hoped coming home would. Instead, the apartment smelled closed-up and musty. Alien. It was as if she were trespassing in a stranger's place, and nothing here belonged to her.

Her throat was parched dry. She needed a drink of water, food, sleep. Sleep most of all—heaven knew, she was too dead beat to think about organizing and arranging and moving yet.

Yet she found herself wandering around, touching all the things that she had once picked out with such painstaking care. Both upstairs and down had been decorated in black and white. The kitchen had the "in" models of pasta machine and cappuccino maker. The wine rack had the correct age and brand of wines, the living room was set up with a bar for entertaining. The bedroom upstairs had nothing out of place, her closet filled with power suits and labels, the shoes predictably lined up like good soldiers.

She sank onto the bed, remembering clearly why the right address, the right place, had been so important to her. A female business executive already had a major strike against her. She'd known image was one of the battles she'd have to fight. At the time, there'd seemed nothing artificial or fake about her choices. Achievement mattered. So did success. She was a believer in self-determination, and working hard was part of that—but so was making no mistakes and leaving nothing to chance. Ambition had been everything to the Abby Stanford who picked out all the cool black-and-white furnishings.

And it was eerily frightening to realize that nothing in the place felt like hers. She no longer knew the woman who'd lived here. She'd always seen truths in black and white. She'd never doubted her judgment of right and wrong.

Gar's face suddenly sneaked into her mind and made the lump in her throat thicken to the size of Alaska. Suddenly cold, she pulled the ebony-and-ivory comforter around her and curled up, thinking that leaving him was the only thing she'd done right in God knows when.

The man was dumb. Dumb enough to take on a woman who couldn't fix a flat tire. So damned dumb that he was attracted to a woman who'd bungled up her life—even if he couldn't see the similarity to his ex-wife. Gar was always going to attract a damsel in distress. He was strong. A natural rescuer. An uncurable white knight.

When a man was that dumb, the honorable thing for a woman to do was remove herself from his presence. He'd said it precisely right. He needed a mate, a wife, the whole shebang. Not just a lover. And for sure, not a woman who couldn't find the right road for herself lately no matter how hard she tried. The only thing she'd excelled at, recently, was failure.

The room was spinning and blurring. She closed her eyes, knowing she was groggy-tired, goofy-tired. But not so tired that she regretted doing the honorable thing. She wasn't failing Gar. He'd find a tough cookie, an equal, if the weak one just left the playing field. She felt good, she told herself.

But tears suddenly burned in her eyes. And her heart ached like a hollow drum as she curled up and tried to sleep.

Midafternoon, Abby pushed open a window to catch some fresh air, and absently noticed a red Taurus pulling up to the curb. She only glanced out for a few seconds.

The crisp air cooled her hot cheeks, but she had no time for a break. In a few short hours, she'd turned the place from pristine-perfect to total chaos. Thankfully, she'd found someone at her old office who wanted the blasted black-and-white furniture, so that albatross was taken care of—or would be, once they came to pick it up the next day. She'd taken care of mail, bills, set up a forwarding address and arranged through the landlord for the utilities to be shut off. Those nuisance chores were done—but then had come the scut work.

Her kitchen cupboards needed emptying. Food boxed up. Clothes sorted through and packed. Lamps and tables and paintings needed hauling to some kind of storage place until she knew where she'd be living next. But everywhere she looked, there was more. Dishes. Towels. Linens, vacuums and hair dryers and cotton balls...how one extremely efficient woman could accumulate so dratted many possessions in seven short years was beyond her.

She'd stopped once, feeling totally overwhelmed, unsure how she was going to tackle it all alone...and wishing it was worse. She couldn't turn a corner without seeing Gar, couldn't open a drawer without thinking of him.

And her mind was on him, not the cherry-red Taurus with rental plates parking in front of the apartment complex. It was unlikely her attention would ever have been distracted by the car, if two women hadn't suddenly climbed out. Two incredibly familiar women.

If the sky started raining bags of gold, Abby couldn't have been more startled. She flew for the door, barefoot, a rag still in her hand, and pelted outside.

"I thought I was hallucinating, for heaven's sake! Are you two out of your minds? What are you *doing* here? For that matter, how did you even know I was in L.A.? And if I've ever seen a pair of bag ladies drag down the neighborhood..."

Damn her sisters. She hated crying worse than root canals. But Paige and Gwen descended on her with open arms and rib-crunching hugs and instant insults, and tears welled up in her eyes, big as puddles.

She looked Paige over first. The youngest in the family had always been the beauty, with her high cheekbones and deep-set eyes and the mane of incredible mink-brown hair. Typically, though, she was dressed in overalls and beat-up tennies, no makeup, her hands a mess of cuts and scrapes from her cameo-carving work. And Paige took the same two seconds to look her over—and immediately started scolding. "We came to help, you dimwit. And we'd have been here earlier if you'd just had brains enough to call us."

"But you can't *be* here. What about the baby—?"

"Well, I'm here courtesy of a breast pump. A little earlier than expected—we thought you were doing this next week, not this one. But that's when I started the breast-pump routine, so the baby's got three days of milk ahead, and anything beyond that Stefan will have to figure out. Trust me, he won't mind. He's so besotted with the baby, the man's thrilled I'm gone. You look like hell," Paige announced.

Gwen jabbed her in the ribs. "She looks a little tired—"

"She looks like total hell."

Gwen, ever the tactful referee, stepped between the two—which gave Abby a better chance to really see her. She was wearing a simple raspberry T-shirt with jeans, her hair was short and sassy, and these days it seemed her gorgeous brown eyes were lit up from a sparkle within. Abby shook her head. "I can't believe you're here any more than Paige. Your honeymoon is barely over, Spense has to resent your coming—"

"Spense insisted I come. He's cool with this, so not to worry. And since we started this marriage with his-and-hers kids, we both figured we'd need a bunch of honeymoons over the long haul. And in the meantime..." Gwen reached the front door first, stepped inside, and took a quick critical look around. "In the meantime, holy kamoly, are we gonna have fun! What a mess."

"Wait, wait, wait." Abby knew her sisters. Both of them were capable of taking charge—and taking over—faster than the spin of a dime. "I still don't understand. How did you even know I was here?"

"Garson," Paige informed her. Wasting no time, she plopped down her tote bag and heeled off her shoes. "I didn't know my Stefan had a jealous bone in his body...until this utterly adorable man with a rich, sexy baritone called in the middle of the night.

Said he got my number from an address book in your condo. I take it that's your Gar?"

"He's not my Gar," Abby said softly.

"Yeah, well." Paige exchanged a glance with Gwen. "It seemed he'd misplaced you. He wanted to know if you were with either of us. Since you obviously weren't, it came down to figuring out where you'd taken off to—and here was the obvious place. You know what?"

"What?" Her mind was still spinning that Gar had called her sisters. She'd never meant him to worry, but she also had never guessed he'd realize she was gone that quickly.

Gwen piped up from the kitchen doorway. "He offered to pay for our plane tickets."

"I don't understand."

Paige answered. "He said you needed some help. Not man help. Sister-type help. I told him thank you, and we'd take care of you and our plane tickets both, not to worry. You've lost five pounds."

"Have not."

"Have, too, and I think it's disgusting. You're too skinny and you have big circles under your eyes, and somehow you still look put-together enough to interview the president. Gwen, dammit, how come I can never manage to look that cool?"

"Because you don't give a damn how you look," Gwen yelled back from the kitchen. "This is my room. You guys stay out. And for the record, I'll take care of dinner. God knows I wouldn't trust either of you near a spatula."

"Well, I can see you need packing boxes, so I might as well start out by making a chore run. You have a list of stuff you need while I'm out? Either of you start any gossip without me and you die. Gwen, don't you lift anything.''

''Will you lay off? I'm not pregnant.'' Gwen's voice was increasingly muffled as she opened and closed cupboards.

''Her stomach's queasy,'' Paige whispered to Abby. ''I think she is. And I'm guessing she and Spense aren't going to settle for less than double the size of brood they have now. Now, about that list...''

The hours passed so fast that Abby could hardly catch her breath. She liked to think she could outwork a draft horse, but her sisters together made a familiar and unbeatable team. In unison, they started singing old dirty rock-and-roll lyrics and fell into fits of giggling in different rooms. Questions were yelled from two stories. The insults never quit. The place started smelling of bleach and disinfectant—and a bubbling French stew from the kitchen.

Gwen served dinner on the carpet in the living room, picnic-style, with crusty Italian bread and a crunchy fresh salad. By then, all three of them were comatose—but not too tired to talk. They caught up on family news, made time to call Mom and Dad, then ran the traditional female gamut from breast feeding and labor to sex and PMS.

Somewhere in the middle of the chatterfest, Gwen jogged back to the kitchen and returned with three paper cups and the fanciest bottle of wine in Abby's rack. ''It's this or aspirin. Every muscle in my body is creaking and groaning,'' she complained.

''You never drink wine,'' Abby reminded her.

''Yeah, Spense teases me that my favorite hard liquor is O.J." She battled with the corkscrew. "But I can suffer through a glass."

"I can suffer through more than one." Paige glanced around. "We've still got one full day's hard work to go, but I think you'll be in pretty good shape after that."

"More than good shape—thanks to you, too," Abby said honestly.

As soon as Gwen had it open, Paige absconded with the bottle and poured her oldest a walloping full glass. "I still think it's stupid to U-Haul your stuff to a rented storage space here. You could truck it east just as well. Plenty of room in the attic, and Vermont's home. Real home. A good place to heal and recharge your juices. Stefan'll feed you chocolate and vodka and fatten you up. You can loll around—"

Gwen interrupted. "You've got a new baby, how would she get any rest? I think she should come home with me. How can you beat a vacation in Florida? Ocean breezes. White sands. Two nephews and a niece to keep you laughing, lots of nice, healing sun. You could stay as long as you wanted—"

"Stop, both of you," Abby said desperately. Putting a thousand miles between herself and Gar hadn't helped. He was still invading her sleep, her dreams, her every waking moment. But it seemed the height of black irony that it was Gar who'd sicced her sisters on her.

He hadn't sent a rescue team. He'd sent a bomb squad.

"Abby..." Paige paused to dip the bottle back in her cup. She'd only taken a sip—and she'd noticed that neither sister had even touched hers. "We can do this easy or we can do it hard, but we're not leaving here—or leaving you—until we get a guarantee in blood that you're okay."

"I'm okay."

"And cows like bubble bath. Talk to us."

Abby dragged a hand through her hair and, because there was obviously no escape, tried talking. "You two...I'm so proud of you both. You're doing so great with your lives, balancing work, kids, house, your men. Love. Neither of you seem to have any doubts about what you want."

"Maybe I've got it straight now," Gwen said, "but two years ago I had a real soul-searching stretch."

"So did I," Paige concurred. "But you were always the one who was dead sure what you wanted, Abby."

"I know. And that's just it. I had it easy, because business always came so naturally to me. I had the ambition and drive, the need to achieve. Only when I was fired...I felt like I'd sold myself a lie. Because everything that mattered so much to me suddenly seemed like a rhinestone instead of a diamond."

"Explain." Gwen refilled her cup this time.

"I just started to realize that what drove me so hard for so long wasn't really ambition. It was that I felt safe, working. I knew the rules. I was good at it. Because when it came down to women's things..." She took a breath. "Gwen, you were always a born mom, fantastic with kids. And Paige, you had your art, but even more than that, you always seemed so sure of yourself as a woman. Independent. Comfortable making your own rules."

"Keep talking," Paige ordered.

"I can't bake cookies. I can't do crafts."

"Well, hell. No wonder you're depressed. Those are giant failures," Paige said dryly.

"I can't do men, either."

"Ah. Now we're getting somewhere," Gwen put in. "You know how often you've given us great advice on men? Like with my Spense—and Paige's Stefan."

"But that's different. I always got along fine with men, working with them, competing with them. I like that whole half of the species, for Pete's sake. But being one of the guys was part of the problem. Because I didn't want to be one of them. I wanted to be *me.* But on the inside, I always felt…flawed. Unfeminine. Like something was missing, because I could never seem to do any of the traditional women things well…*why* are you two looking at each other?"

"Is she talking about sex?" Paige asked Gwen.

"Were you born yesterday? How long have we been sisters? Of course she's talking about sex," Gwen said impatiently. And then, to Abby: "You're a doofus for not telling us this before. I watched you push away every guy who tried to get too close. I just didn't understand why. So. You were especially scared of screwing up when the lights went off—how'd that go with Gar?"

"Fine."

"Clarify *fine.*"

"All right. It went damn well splendiferous." Cripes, the two of them were more relentless than hounds. And the wine, Abby knew, was starting to go straight to her head. "That part was wonderful. But it doesn't mean I have the first clue how to make a real relationship work. Or that I'm good for him. And lately it seems like I've failed at everything I've tried to do—''

''Get specific,'' Paige ordered. ''What specifically have you failed at? Besides making cookies.''

She didn't know how to sum it up except simply. ''Being strong.''

''Well, get a noose,'' Paige said to Gwen. ''That's certainly a hanging offense. Everyone else in the universe, of course, is always strong all the time.''

''You don't understand. He had someone before. A woman whose signature tune was 'Lean on Me.' It's the last thing he needs. Another woman who doesn't have her head straight, who can't seem to even make up her mind where she's going next...''

''I get it now. Because you're in the process of making a major life change, it means you're no good to anyone right now. Worthless. Useless. A total turkey. No one anyone could love.''

''You're making fun.'' Abby gulped down a little more wine. ''But there's more to the picture.''

''So tell us.''

''Honesty matters to him. Gar's just the kind of man who values integrity to the bone. And honesty seemed to be the one thing I couldn't give him. I just couldn't bring myself to tell him that I'd been fired, or this whole failure thing I've been going through...''

''Why?'' Paige asked bluntly. ''What do you think would happen, what's the worst-case scenario you can think of, if you laid a little of that honesty at his feet?''

Abby wrapped her arms around her knees and held on tight. ''I don't know. He could lose his respect for me. He could change his mind about ever caring for me. I don't know how to explain this, but everything was different with him. With him, I was more...the woman I wanted to be. But I never believed he saw the woman I really was."

When Gwen started to speak, Paige put a quelling hand on her arm. Her voice turned sober, quiet. "So we're down to pay dirt. You think you've been lying to him all this time? Fooling him that maybe you're a better or a different woman than you really are?"

Abby swallowed. "Yes. Exactly."

"Then I think you're being selfish, sis," Paige said frankly.

"Selfish?" Abby had been wallowing in guilt about everything she'd done wrong from here to Sunday, but selfishness was the one sin her conscience seemed clear of.

"Uh-huh. It's obvious that the man seriously cares. He would hardly have tracked us down if he didn't. Maybe breaking it off is the best thing, but it'd be selfish not to talk to him first. You think he's fallen in love with this mistaken image of an incredibly wonderful and loving woman. God knows how he could have gotten an insane idea like that, but the point is...you left him hanging."

A fist squeezed her heart so tight she could hardly breathe. "I *never* meant to do that. Hurting him is exactly what I was trying not to do in any way—"

"Well, you did. For all you know, he's sitting there in Tahoe, blaming himself for whatever went wrong. If you really want to let him off the hook, the kindest thing would be to lay some of this stuff on the line. Give him the truth about what a terrible, hopeless failure of a woman you are. You'd be giving him a reason to be glad it's over."

Abby clawed a hand through her hair again. "Sheesh. I never once thought of it that way, that I was being selfish."

When Abby's head was averted, Paige delivered a high five to Gwen—but she kept talking in that sincere-as-a-judge voice. "Sometimes it takes a sister to deliver the cold hard truth. We hate to be hard on you, but there it is."

"No, no. I'm glad you were hard on me. I needed it...." Abby climbed unsteadily to her feet, her mind so wine-muzzy she was weaving. "But I wouldn't try taking that con routine on the road."

"Con?" Gwen was the best at expressing innocent shock at the accusation.

"I saw the high five. I watched you two pouring wine down my throat. Did you forget I'm the oldest? I taught you two everything you ever tried to pull on me. Thanks, you two. I love you. But for heaven's sakes, let's call this quits and hit the sack."

Both sisters said, "Abby..." in unison.

"I'm going back to Tahoe. I'm going to see him. I promise."

It was all she had to say to squelch any further serious talk. The three of them mass-exodused toward the stairs and bed, all so beat they were stumbling on their feet. When the lights were out, though, Abby couldn't stop thinking about her return to Tahoe.

And what she needed to say to Gar.

Chapter Fourteen

It was late afternoon when Abby turned into the lodge parking lot, her pulse thumping with nerves and her palms slick with anxiety. When she parked the car and climbed out, the wind tore at her face, mean as a wolf's teeth. A fresh snow glinted on the ski slopes, glistening like a glaze of whipped cream.

As if she owned the place and had a vested interest, her gaze automatically counted the number of cars and bodies milling around. A good cash day for Gar. The true hard-case skiers went manic after a fresh snowfall, and they couldn't care less about a little cold. Neither did she. She seemed to have hopelessly lost her heart to Tahoe.

If she had a critical problem with cold feet, it had nothing to do with the weather.

Head down, jaw firmed, she forced her coward's

cold feet to make fast tracks toward the main lobby of the lodge. She was well aware her sisters believed they'd talked her into this, and in Abby's unbiased opinion, Cinderella had had *nice* sisters compared to hers. Both her younger siblings had a shameful ruthless streak—calling her selfish and unkind, using guilt to manipulate her into seeing Gar again.

They loved her. So much that Abby didn't have the heart to tell them that they'd never talked her into anything.

She'd always intended to come back. Always planned on seeing Gar again. Abby had never failed to own up to her mistakes before, and she couldn't have lived with herself if she ran away from this one. She'd hurt Gar by her failure to be honest with him. There would always have come a point when that had to be made right, no matter what it cost her…no matter what it lost her.

The Los Angeles trip might have postponed this confrontation with Gar, but that part of her life also needed a period at the end of the sentence. The last of her ties there were now severed, and the few things she'd put in storage could stay there indefinitely. L.A. was where she'd started making the mistakes that were still haunting her now. Going back, rubbing her nose in it, had made those mistakes infinitely clearer. More to the point, that entire distraction was now out of the way.

She opened the door to the lobby. The blast of warm air was as comforting and soothing as hope.

But this wasn't about hope. It was about taking a risk so scary that her stomach was clenched in panic-size knots. The taste in her mouth had the flavor of dread. She thought of the black-and-white cameo her sister had made her and reminded herself—for the dozenth time—that some things *were* black-and-white. There was no compromising the kinds of truth that really mattered.

And love, she'd irrevocably discovered, was one of those truths.

She ditched her jacket on the coat rack off the lobby, ran a fast brush through her hair and smoothed the red sweater she was wearing over jeans. The casual attire was a far cry from the dress-for-success maxim she used to live by. But that was her old life. And for Gar, especially this time, no prettying up the package would do. She needed to be just herself.

As she strode through the lobby toward the stairs, Simpson screeched an exuberant greeting and a few others yelled out hellos. Having a familiar face was an advantage; no one stopped her or asked where she was going or why. She flashed back a smile for everyone, but her heart was slamming, *Don't you fail this. No matter what you failed before, you have to do this right. You have to find a way.*

Late afternoon, Gar was likely to be in his office, busy, but taking care of paperwork, rather than people problems. She'd considered his usual work routine before choosing the time. If she mucked up, she could escape quickly—and so could he, with the ready-made excuse of a piled-up desk if he wanted her gone.

She was badly afraid that a little absence had given him time to think. Time to consider that his life was a lot more peaceful without her in it. Maybe it was too late to ask him to listen. Maybe...he wouldn't want to see her at all.

That dread pulse was kicking hard as she rounded the corner into his office. At a glance, she noticed the inner office door was closed—which was definitely peculiar. Gar never closed that door; he felt too strongly about being accessible to his staff. But Robb was typically installed at his desk, neck-deep in spreadsheets and payroll and papers. The white teeth of a grin showed through his bushy black beard. "Hey. You've been missed, ma'am."

"What, you couldn't find anyone else to fight with for a couple of days?"

"No one who's as much fun to argue with as you. Good to see you back."

"Thanks." She motioned toward the closed door. "I just wanted to see Gar for a few minutes, but I don't want to interrupt him if he's busy or in the middle of something important—"

"He's in there." Something gleamed in Robb's eyes beyond a welcoming hello. "And trust me, it's a perfect time for you to go in."

When she hesitated—surely Gar had the door closed for a reason?—Robb bounced out of his office chair and, thoroughly startling her, draped a brotherly arm around her shoulders. For a couple seconds, she was so curious about what motivated the sudden, comradelike hug that she wasn't conscious of being steered. As silent as a mouse, Robb turned the knob on Gar's office door. He didn't precisely shove her—more pushed her inside. By the time she realized the door was click-closing behind her, she was inescapably in.

Her first thought was of murdering Gar's executive assistant. Maybe via boiling in oil, or red ants. Plotting a gruesome murder for Robb would have given her a great deal of satisfaction, but at that precise moment, she couldn't indulge the time for it.

Gar was in his office. But he wasn't alone.

Although Janet was standing at the window, her face turned away, Abby easily recognized his ex-wife. The perfume scent pervading the office was sweet, soft spring flowers instead of Obsession, but the thick froth of brunette curls was easily recognizable. Her showcase figure was decked out in a lace blouse and slim skirt, nothing sultry or low-cut this time. Abby recognized well enough when a woman had worked to put together an image. This one was vulnerable, not seductive. And so was the voice.

Abby was only frozen in the doorway for a few seconds. Escaping at the speed of light—and preferably before either of them noticed her—was her first and obvious choice of action. Whatever her plan for conversation and confrontation with Gar, this obviously wasn't the time. She'd never have chosen to awkwardly intrude on a meeting between him and ex-wife. And none of those obvious conclusions took more than a few milliseconds to register in her mind, but in the same heart-hiccuping few moments, she heard that helplessly sweet, soft voice.

"I can't make it alone, Gar. I never could. I just could never be strong the way you are, and you know I can't turn to my family. You're the only one I could possibly ask for help."

"Look, Janet. It's not that I'm unwilling to help you, but if the reason you're in debt is because of drugs again—"

"I'm not using anything now. It was just a small setback, and I'm trying as hard as I know how...but

I need help, Gar. I'll never ask you for money again, I swear. But I'm in trouble, and I just can't handle it alone..."

Gar was also standing at the window, rubbing the back of his neck, when he suddenly pivoted around and saw her.

Damn. Abby'd known before this that he owned a corner of her heart, but it was as if she hadn't breathed the whole time she was in L.A. Not air that mattered. Not the kind of air that sustained life.

Whatever he'd been about to say or do, he stopped moving entirely when he spotted her. He was just wearing a gray wool sweater and comfortable gray cords, but she inhaled the look of him as if they'd been separated for months. Love. She could have sworn she saw love in his eyes, deep and dark as a river, and surely he couldn't look at her with that kind of intimate intensity if he hadn't missed her?

But then he shifted on his feet, and his gaze shot back to his ex-wife. All emotion seemed to be vacuumed out of his expression. She'd seen that stoic look before, seen the harsh stress lines carved in his face when Gar was braced for trouble. And beneath his skier's ruddy tan was a gray tiredness that came too damn close to matching his sweater.

His ex-wife's words pounced back into her mind. *I need help, Gar...I'm in trouble...*

Abby knew perfectly well that trouble didn't scare him. Gar could probably manage a couple of small countries in his spare time. But she also knew he had a couple of nasty Achilles' heels, namely his sense of honor and that disgracefully archaic rescuer streak he had about women.

Janet spun around suddenly then, and spotted her, too. Abby's mouth opened. The only conceivable thing to do was apologize quickly for interrupting them and leave.

Only...he needed her. She wasn't positive where the strong feminine instinct came from, when she'd never felt confident about trusting her woman's instincts before. And it wasn't like she doubted that he could cope. It was just...she simply couldn't desert a man with a flat tire in a blizzard in the middle of the night.

"I didn't realize there was anyone in here but Gar," she said swiftly.

"Well, you're interrupting a private conversation." When Janet swiveled around completely, Abby caught a better look at her. That beautiful face was more gaunt than the last time she'd seen her; the pupils were dilated and huge, the long, slim, pretty hands were trembling slightly. Abby had no way to judge how much might be a manipulative act and how much was real, but this wasn't a happy woman. And she thought, somewhere in that face, in those eyes, was a woman he'd once loved.

"I realized that right away, and I'm sorry for interrupting," Abby said carefully, "but I also couldn't help but overhear what you were saying. You're in some kind of trouble? There's something you need our help with?"

Our. Her man needed big guns, and the best she'd come up with was a paltry three-letter word. Because it simply wasn't enough, she crossed the room to Gar and claimed his hand, just the heart's breadth of a quick squeeze, but she hoped enough to communicate a gesture of alliance.

"This has nothing to do with you," Janet said curtly.

"That could well be true, but if you've got a problem, it wouldn't make much sense to turn down another listening ear.... You look like you could use a cup of tea or coffee."

"I don't want a drink."

"Okay." Without thinking, she took a protective step in front of Gar. "I had the impression what you wanted was money."

"I'm in debt." Those big, haunted eyes zoomed behind her. There was no question about who she wanted to talk to—and it wasn't another woman. "Terribly serious debt—"

Abby gently interrupted. "And it sounds as if you're scared, as well. Pretty hard not to be afraid—if you've got drugs controlling your life."

"I just had a small setback—"

"Uh-huh." She'd already seen the dilated pupils, the shaky hands. "I'm sorry, Janet. I mean that. I can't claim to really understand, because I haven't had the problem, but I've had friends and people I worked with who did. I heard them say it more than once... you can't fight it until you're seriously ready."

"I *am* ready. I just got in some financial trouble—"

"So you said." Abby sucked in a lungful of courage. It was going to take some extra oxygen to come out with these lies. She'd sworn she'd never fib or evasively color the truth around Gar ever again. Worse yet, she was miserably conscious of intruding on something he might well feel was none of her business. "Janet, we both feel that money is no way to help you, because we're afraid of what you'll use it for. If you want help, real help, you've got it. Gar has already agreed with me that we'd be willing to help you with another rehab try. There are lots of places with different ideas on treatments, if the first one didn't work for you. Counseling, as well. And that offer's good whenever you're ready to take it. But that's it."

"Gar!" Janet turned to him with welling tears. "I came to talk to you, not her. And I know you wouldn't turn me out in the street—"

Abby couldn't see his face, but a hand—a big, heavy hand—reached down and cuffed her wrist as securely as a handcuff. "Then you'd better believe it," he told his ex-wife, "because it was Abby's idea to do anything. Not mine. If I were you, I'd be thanking her."

"I don't need counseling—"

"Neither of us said you did. Only that if you needed financial help, that's the only form we're offering it. And that's the only way it's going to be, Janet."

An awkward silence followed. His ex-wife stared at him, and then abruptly turned around and grabbed her coat and purse. She let herself out, with shoulders proud-straight and eyes filled with dramatic, tragic tears.

When the door finally closed, the office was quieter than a cave for several moments. And then Gar heaved an exhausted sigh. "Every encounter I have with her makes me feel like I've been hit by a moving train. Not exactly a restful way to end an afternoon."

"No." He was still holding her hand. Abby wasn't sure if he realized it. "Um, Gar?"

"What?"

"It's okay to kill me now." She felt his eyes on her face, but guilt was weighing her eyelids down so heavily that the best she could do was stare at his desk.

"Why would I want to kill you?"

A kindergartner could have figured it out, but she filled him in. "For interfering. For coming up with those lies. For making her think it was your idea on the rehab. For volunteering your money that you may not have wanted volunteered, for that matter."

"Abby...I've admitted before that I have a hard time being tough with her," he said quietly.

"I know you do."

His voice was low, slow, gentle. "And you already know I get disgusted with myself for not handling it better. I'm working on it. But for the record, I would have gotten the tough words said, if you hadn't been here. There was no way I was giving her cash to support her drug habit, and she's long run out of excuses to show up at my door. But I wouldn't have said it tactfully—or half as well as you did. You not only did the right thing, you did it for me. And with me."

"You're really not aggravated with me." She had to look at his face, then, to be absolutely sure. His left hand came up to tuck a strand of hair behind her ear. From the intensity in his expression, his ex-wife was no longer remotely on his mind.

"It's about damn time you came back from L.A."

"You sicced my sisters on me."

"Yeah, I did." His eyes were true blue. She'd never seen less than total honesty in his eyes, in his face, anywhere around him. "When you left, you were upset," he explained, "and I didn't think you wanted to see me."

"Well, I want to see you now, Cameron—if you can clear your decks for a few minutes. But after that nerve-racking scene with your ex-wife, maybe you just might want a little space and time to yourself—"

"The hell I do."

Faster than a speeding bullet, he pulled on her hand, yanked open the door and barged past Robb. "I'll be upstairs. Tell the switchboard not to put through any calls. If the place burns down, handle it."

"Will do."

A number of people were spilling out of the elevator. Gar ducked around them and took the back stairs—two at a time—and since he seemed disinclined to relinquish her hand, Abby had to hustle to keep up with him. By the time they were inside his lodge apartment and he'd thrown the dead bolt, she was breathless from their panting-fast job.

"You hungry?" he asked her.

Hungry? The last thing in the universe on her mind was food. "I— No."

"Can't help it. I'm starved. I don't think I've had a real meal since you left—but I'm afraid there's nothing in the fridge but cold pizza and maybe some beer and cola."

She hadn't come to eat, but nothing could coax the man to sit still. He installed her, feet up, on the couch, and then kept putting things in front of her. Napkins, silverware, nuked pizza, pop. And a marshmallow sundae with chocolate ice cream. Served with dinner, damn him.

"Gar," she said a half-dozen times. But each time, he responded with a question about what she wanted next. Nuked pizza wasn't remotely on her list of desires. "Cameron, would you *listen* to me for a second, for heaven's sake?" And out it spilled. "I was fired."

Gar felt like a wide receiver who'd waited three quarters to finally get his hands on a forward pass. He could see the goal posts, smell that a touchdown was possible...if he just didn't do anything damn stupid, like fumbling the ball. "So...you were fired," he repeated casually, as if she hadn't finally confessed that monster secret after all these weeks.

"Yeah. From an advertising firm. McVey and Rhettiker." Abby stopped to swallow. Although he doubted she was aware of it, she'd devoured three slices of the pizza, as if she hadn't had food in days. "I was on their management team for seven years. Up for the CEO's job when he retired. They gave it to someone else and booted me out."

"Impossible to feel sympathy for people that dumb." He handed her another napkin, studying her face, remembering her expression when she'd edged in front of him and taken on Janet. She'd perceived that he needed her, and for Abby, that was ample justification to step in front of a lion. There'd been naked nerves in her eyes then, and there were raw, vulnerable nerves in her dark eyes now. She thought she was risking another lion. One that could turn on her.

She gulped down the ginger ale, her face as pale as parchment. "They weren't dumb, Gar. And I don't know whether they were right or wrong. I just know that I felt ashamed, like I was a failure. And that's why I didn't tell you before. Because I didn't want you to see me that way."

"Pride," Gar said.

"I've always had too much of it," she admitted. "And the thing was...being fired forced me to see that I'd been making some huge mistakes. I'd made my career my whole life. Valued success like it was the Holy Grail. So I was trying to fix myself, Gar. Redefine who I was, turn myself into a different kind of woman—"

"The cookies," he murmured. "The gourmet feast for the marines, all those crafts..."

"I wasn't trying to fool you into thinking I was a genetic cross between Martha Stewart and June Cleaver. Or fib to you about my background in business. None of that was about lack of honesty. I didn't know what the truth *was.* I wanted to erase the old workaholic Abby Stanford off the map, make sure I never made those same mistakes again, to *be* seriously different. Only I seemed to be failing at everything new I tried." Abby gulped one last sip of soda and set the glass down. "And in middle of all that confusion trying to change myself, I met you. Found you. Fell in love with you."

"You love me." Trust Abby to drop a bomb while she was impatiently wiping her hands on a napkin.

"Dammit, I wanted...serenity."

"Serenity," Gar echoed, as he removed the plate from her lap. Then the napkin. Then the spoon she'd decided to pick up and cling to—as if it were a weapon that could save her from lions.

And then he claimed her hands, while she was still extremely busy talking.

"That was always the missing piece. I loved business, the challenge, the ninety-mile-an-hour pace. It just never occurred to me that I was running so fast that I was also running away. I wasn't at peace with myself. I was never comfortable with myself as a woman. I respected Abby Stanford on the job, but the things that mattered—whether she knew how to love, whether anyone could conceivably love the flawed human being underneath, that serenity thing—were never there." She frowned abruptly. "Where on earth are you dragging me off to *now*, Cameron?"

"There's just one room in the apartment that you haven't seen."

"You may not want me in there."

"Trust me. I do."

"You may not. You may kick me out. There are still some things I seriously need to tell you—"

"You think I'm trying to cut off communication? I want you to keep talking." But in the middle of the hall, he pinned her against the wall for a kiss. It just wouldn't wait. He'd thought he'd lost her. That fear clanging in his pulse was lessening now, seeping away, but touching her healed and reassured him as nothing else could have. He inhaled her taste, her scent, her textures, in that kiss...and she didn't seem to mind.

Her hands skated up his arms and then wrapped winsomely, yearningly, naturally, around his neck. She kissed like sweetness and sunshine. She kissed like a power-packed package of sheer concentrated love. She kissed like a sexy, sultry woman who couldn't wait a second longer for her man.

God knew how he'd lived without her before this.

She came up for air. Eventually. Tenderly stroked his cheek, his jaw. "That was one of the things I wanted to explain," she said huskily. "That I didn't want you kissing any women that you didn't feel proud to kiss. That was why I was so shook up when I fell in love with you. Everywhere I turned, I seemed to be struggling and bumbling. I didn't want you stuck with another dependent type who needed rescuing. I wanted you to know I was strong enough to stand tall next to you."

"I never doubted your strength, Abby. And I was proud of you the first time I saw you determined to lick a flat tire in a blizzard. Every time I needed you, you've been there for me. I've worried it the other way. That you never seemed to need me."

"But I do." Her voice was softer than a spring wind. "You're my serenity, Garson Cameron."

She was still talking when they reached his bedroom. The silky shadows provided more than enough illumination for him to pull off her red sweater. Her arms curled back around him even before he could lift her to the four-poster.

"It took me so long to see it. I was so busy trying to change, trying to hide my flaws from you—only it never worked. You kept catching me at my worst. You figured out my love for business. You already know I'm never going to master laid-back and lazy in this lifetime."

"You sit still about as well as a wet cat," he agreed.

"And there it is. That smile of yours. Damn you, Cameron, you accepted me before I did. Something is terribly wrong with your judgment. You always seemed to *like* the parts of me that I thought were all wrong."

"Love," he corrected her. And unzipped her jeans.

"That's when I figured it out—that there was no truth I had to hide from you. That serenity, that naturalness, was always there. I'm happy when I'm with you. Happy on the inside." Her breath caught. "But I don't know how you feel about hooking up with an unemployed, fired ex–ad exec who's still struggling for a few of those serious life answers—"

"I was ready to weld a ring on your finger a month ago." He smoothed back her hair, loving the look in her eyes. "And I think that's what marriage is about, Abby. Having someone you can bring those struggles home to. I don't know any answers that last. What lasts is finding someone you can grow with, learn with, share honestly with. I *love* you."

"And oh, I love you back. Like I never dreamed I could love." She reached for him. Her touch was loving, her mouth claiming his with fierce, evocative, alluring kisses that communicated promises—and need. The last of their clothes were peeled away. The sheets were cold, but not for long. The pillows were soft, but not as rose-soft as her skin, her mouth, her hands.

He understood what she'd said about serenity, but just then, restfulness was the last thing he wanted to arouse in Abby. The first time he met her, he sensed she was a 200% woman, a woman with a mountain of love in her, who gave 200% when she loved...and who needed a man who'd give her 200% back.

The flint-and-tinder chemistry was easy; they'd always sparked fire whenever they touched. But this time the heat had the richness of commitment licking flames around both of them, burning desire hotter, freeing both of them to a different plane of honesty. Desire was a seal. Their shared vulnerability both a joy and a promise.

When it was over, he snuggled her close, touching her, loving her, until both of them got their breath back. And then he murmured, "What time do you think the marriage-license place opens in the morning?"

She chuckled softly. "You sound in a rush to make an honest woman out of me."

"You were always an honest woman. You were the only one who didn't know it, Stanford—but I *am* in a hustle to change your last name."

"Hmmm." She scooched on top of his chest—pinning him beneath her extremely effectively. "What do you think about having a houseful of little Camerons?"

"I think our kids will be hellions to raise, exhausting overachievers with way too much energy and ambition to ever keep 'em down. Afraid they're doomed, with a double dose of those genes coming from both parents."

"It's a terrifying thought, isn't it?"

He saw the gleam in her eyes. There was nothing Abby loved more than a nice, terrifying challenge....and Gar suspected that would only get worse as the years passed. On the mom front, he already knew what their children were in for. She'd not only be a 200% mother, but the kind of nurturer to instill confidence and courage because she intimately knew those life roads so well.

Her fear of failing wasn't going to disappear overnight, Gar understood, and her faith in herself needed building. But that was good work for a man who loved her, ideal work for a life mate to share.

And with her in his life, there wasn't anything he couldn't imagine them conquering. Together.

Epilogue

Abby stepped back to take a critical look in the antique mirror. Temporarily the veil looked drunk—it was a real pistol to make it hang straight. Yet she paused, the veil forgotten, when she caught the full-length reflection of the dress.

The cream gown had been her grandmother's wedding dress, then her mother's, and both her sisters had worn it for their weddings. The style was old-fashioned, with a sweetheart bodice and puffed sleeves, the satin fabric softened with lace and seed pearls—and the look of it brought tears to her eyes. She'd never felt comfortable near anything old-fashioned before. For so long, she'd feared she'd never find her "place" between traditional woman's roles and all the complex, emerging new roles for women of today.

But that had been before she met Gar. Before she understood that the role of love in her life had opened up an endless box of choices—and the challenge to be any kind of woman she wanted to be.

Outside the open window, lilacs were bursting, hyacinths perfuming the spring air. Paige had insisted the wedding be here—home, the Vermont homestead that had been in the Stanford family since the 1800s. More tradition, and Gar had taken to the idea as warmly as Abby had. She'd just leaned forward to start fussing and fixing the veil when she heard a sudden knock at the door.

Paige burst in, then Gwen. "Mom sent us to tell you the minister just got here...and your groom hasn't had the good sense to take a powder yet."

"He'd better not," Abby chuckled. And then her smile softened. "Oh, you two. You look so beautiful!"

Paige, under duress, was spiffed up in an elegant coral dress—decorated with a diaper on one shoulder, as she patted the baby. Gwen looked just as breathtaking in coral, although her dress had required some fancy sewing to accommodate the watermelon-size bulge in her tummy.

Abby felt more moisture welling up in her eyes. Not helping her at all, their eyes filled, too. "You two can't even imagine what you mean to me," she said softly.

"Yikes, don't you start," Paige scolded gruffly. "I only wear mascara once in a year, and if you make it run, I swear I'm going down the aisle with black eyes." Her gruff tone softened. "I love you, sis."

"Me, too." Gwen reached her first. Then Paige. The tangled arms and loving hugs reminded Abby of all the secrets the sisters had shared. So much of what she valued about family came from them. Her sisters had indelibly taught her what women could bring to each other, what support really was. They had never failed to be a source of unconditional love.

"I have something to tell you two," Abby said.

"Oh, God. You're not backing out of the wedding. If you do, I swear I'm adopting Gar—with Stefan's permission, of course."

"Hey, I've got first dibs on adopting him—assuming it's okay with Spense," Gwen shot back.

"No, he's mine, all mine." Abby laughed. But even thinking about Gar made her feel a giant swell of radiance from deep inside her. For a moment she recalled the ivory-and-onyx cameo Paige had made for her. The cameo had always seemed to glow from a light on the inside. There was a time she'd thought she'd never find the truth that mattered in her life, never know that glow of inner serenity that came from confidence. That time was gone. She'd never felt so alive—or so full of love. She smiled at her sisters. "This is a good secret, something that even Gar doesn't know yet—"

Gwen rolled her eyes at Paige. "As if we didn't guess you were pregnant."

"You knew?"

"We've been there. And you've got the look—especially when you look at that man of yours. And we couldn't be happier for you in a thousand million years." Gwen threw her arms around her again. Paige and the baby crushed closer to share in yet another hug—and another round of tears.

Gwen mopped them all up with handkerchiefs,

straightened her veil, and then bossily herded Paige and the baby toward the door. "If we don't get moving, we're going to be late for the last wedding in the family, for Pete's sake. We're leaving. This instant. But I just have to tell you...you're the most beautiful bride that ever existed in the universe, sis. And trust me, I have no bias in this."

"My opinion's completely objective on this, too," Paige affirmed. "You're spectacularly beautiful, Abby. You couldn't possibly be more perfect."

When her sisters hustled out and left her alone for a moment, Abby thought, No, not perfect. Not even close to perfect. She'd always gone after everything she valued 200%, making her successes nice, but her mistakes inevitably giant ones. Once, that had made her fear failure—but not anymore.

Gar seemed to love her exactly as she was. And there was this strange thing that came from the confidence of feeling well and truly loved. She could hardly wait for all the challenges ahead—both the good and the bad.

She took a second to compose herself—and then couldn't wait any longer. Downstairs was a man she wanted nothing more than to vent 500% of her love on. She swooped up her train and walked out the door to Gar.

* * * * *

April 1997 **WHAT TO DO ABOUT BABY**
by Martha Hix (SE #1093)

When a handsome lawyer showed up on Carolyn Grant's doorstep with a toddler in tow, she didn't know what to think. Suddenly, she had a little sister she'd never known about...and a *very* persistent man intent on making Caro his own....

June 1997 **HIS DAUGHTER'S LAUGHTER**
by Janis Reams Hudson (SE #1105)

Carly Baker came to widower Tyler Barnett's ranch to help his fragile daughter—and connected emotionally with the caring father and tenderhearted girl. But when Tyler's interfering in-laws began stirring up trouble, would Carly be forced to give up the man and child she loved?

And in August, be sure to check out...

ALISSA'S MIRACLE
by
Ginna Gray (SE#1117)

He'd told her that he could never have a child, and lovely widow Alissa Kirkpatrick was so in love with enigmatic Dirk Matheson that she agreed to a childless marriage. Until the pregnancy test proved positive....

THAT'S MY BABY!
Sometimes, bringing up baby can bring surprises...and showers of love.

Look us up on-line at: http://www.romance.net TMBA-A